A MEASURE OF MAYHEM

CAFE CRIMES COZY MYSTERY

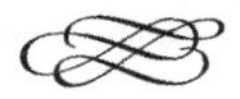

SIMONE STIER

A Measure of Mayhem

A Cafe Crimes Cozy Mystery
Simone Stier

Cover art by Mariah Sinclair

DEDICATION

To amateur sleuths everywhere …

CHAPTER 1

I stood shivering in the winter morning chill, my breath puffing out in little clouds as I fumbled with the poles of my canopy. Lake Magnolia stretched out before me, a mirror of steely gray reflecting the slowly lightening sky. The whole scene would've been postcard-perfect if I wasn't fighting a losing battle with an inanimate object at seven in the morning.

"Come on, you glorified umbrella," I muttered, yanking on a stubborn pole. "Cooperate!"

The metal frame gave a sudden pop, and I stumbled backward, nearly taking out my carefully arranged boxes of coffee supplies. So much for grace under pressure. At least a few of the other vendors were too busy setting up their booths to witness my stellar handyman skills in action.

I straightened up, brushing off my parka and what was left of my dignity. When I'd decided to participate in Magnolia Grove's annual Frost Fest, I'd pictured myself serenely dispensing steaming cups of hot coffee to grateful, frost-bitten festival attendees. I hadn't factored in the joys of outdoor booth assembly in near-freezing temperatures.

"Need a hand there, Parker?"

I turned to see Whit Hawthorne—Magnolia Grove's dashing historian and my recently minted boyfriend—approaching, looking unfairly put-together for this early hour. His cheeks were rosy from the cold, and he wore a knit cap that made him look like some kind of rugged small-town lumberjack. It was irritatingly charming.

"Whit! My knight in flannel armor," I said, gesturing to the half-standing canopy. "Feel like wrestling with some poles?"

He chuckled, pulling me in for a quick kiss. "I do enjoy a good canopy-wrestling session before breakfast."

I savored the moment, still not quite used to this new aspect of our relationship. Whit had been my partner in crime-solving since I'd arrived in Magnolia Grove at the end of summer, his encyclopedic knowledge of the town's history proving invaluable in our investigations. It had taken three murder cases and a near-death experience for us to finally admit our feelings went beyond friendship.

Working together, we managed to get the canopy up and the fold-out table in position without further incident. I turned my attention to the next challenge: powering up my coffee station and outdoor space heater—my best defense against the chill.

"Looks like we need to hook up to the festival's generator," I said, eyeing the distance between my booth and the hulking gas-powered energy source fifty yards away.

Whit nodded, already reaching for the coiled extension cord. "I'll run this over."

I watched as Whit expertly unwound the heavy-duty cable, his movements smooth and assured. Even something as mundane as electrical work looked graceful when Whit did it. He plugged the cord into the generator.

"Earth to Parker …" Whit's amused voice snapped me out of my reverie as he walked back toward me. "Unless you're planning to serve iced coffee, we should probably plug this in." He held up the other end of the cable.

My cheeks warmed, and not just from the cold. "Right. Sorry. Just … supervising."

Whit's eyes sparkled flirtatiously. "Of course. Excellent supervision technique."

Together, we secured the cable to avoid trip hazards. As Whit plugged in the coffee machines and heater, I appreciated how seamlessly we worked together, whether solving crimes or setting up for one of Magnolia Grove's many festivals. Did I mention this small town definitely loved its celebrations?

Whit gave a pleased nod. "Now you can keep Magnolia Grove caffeinated without freezing."

I grinned, flipping the switch on my heater and then the espresso machine. It hummed to life, a comforting sound in the crisp morning air. "My hero."

"So, ready for your first Frost Fest?"

I snorted. "Oh, absolutely. I live for the opportunity to freeze my toes off while caffeinating half the town. It's a lifelong dream come true."

Whit's eyes crinkled at the corners. "Come on, Parker. Where's your festive spirit?"

"Buried under three layers of thermals." I held my hands toward the heater. Despite my griping, there was something enchanting about the quiet lake and the promise of the day ahead.

"Well," Whit said, rubbing his gloved hands together, "I'm going to help Clyde get the stage set up. Don't brew up too much trouble while I'm gone, okay?"

I grinned and blew him a playful kiss. "No promises, Hawthorne. Trouble's my specialty, as you know ..."

As Whit walked away, chuckling, I turned back to my booth and surveyed my little outdoor coffee kingdom with satisfaction. I brewed up a fresh pot of a rich dark roast with nutty undertones, then set out my jars of coffee grounds for my latest drink concoction, the Minted Mayhem Latte. I used a medium roast blend with hints of vanilla for the base, then added refreshing peppermint syrup, topping off the creamy foam with a drizzle of decadent chocolate. I inhaled deeply, savoring the moment. Despite the early hour and chilly temperatures, I felt a buzz of excitement for the day ahead. This Frost Fest might just be fun, after all. Or maybe it was just the coffee.

Some more vendors began to arrive, their chatter carrying across the still surface of the lake. I joined in as they passed my booth, exchanging warm greetings and offering even warmer lattes. But the harmony was short-lived as a commotion from behind the parking area announced the arrival of one Lauren Yancey, owner of Feta & Friends, Magnolia Grove's artisanal cheese shop.

The overly serious businesswoman marched across the lightly snow-covered grass, her designer boots crunching with each determined step. Her expertly highlighted blonde shoulder-length hair was straightened to perfection. In her arms, she clutched a sleek leather portfolio and what looked like a very expensive cheese board. Trailing behind her like ducklings were her two employees. Ethan Fontaine, the genius behind the artisanal cheeses, struggled with a large cart containing a bunch of gear for the booth setup. His sculpted features and chestnut curls gave him a European male model flair. Sophia Quinn, Lauren's dutiful assistant, juggled a box of materials and a long cardboard cylinder. The professionally dressed petite brunette exuded nervous energy that screamed: "eager to please."

"Good morning, Lauren and crew," I called out, lifting a paper cup. "Care for some mint latte to warm you up?"

Lauren barely glanced my way. "You know I don't drink useless calories, Parker."

Ethan and Sophia, catching my eye, gave apologetic nods. I could almost see them salivating at the thought of a toasty, warm drink.

"First, we need to get set up!" Lauren barked at them, surveying their booth space. "And Sophia, let's not overcomplicate things. This isn't one of your escape room designs."

"You got it, Lauren," Sophia said, seemingly unfazed by Lauren's harsh demeanor.

Ethan stopped the cart and began unloading the items.

Yancey yelled out, "No, no, no! Our display is going over there." She pointed to the ground ten feet away from where Ethan had started his project. "Do I have to do everything myself?"

"Lauren, I'm a cheese-maker, not a roadie," Ethan muttered.

Lauren Yancey was a bit of a puzzle. We shared a similar backstory—escaping the big city's chaos for Magnolia Grove's small-town charm. I'd traded my popular true-crime podcast for a quieter life, while she'd left high-powered finance to open Feta & Friends with unbridled enthusiasm, sending ripples through our small town.

On paper, we should have been kindred spirits—two city transplants seeking a fresh start. But Lauren's icy demeanor only embellished her meticulous business acumen. All business, little warmth. My attempts at friendly neighborliness were met, on good days, with tight-lipped smiles and cursory waves. Even when I placed a sizable order of mascarpone and ricotta for a new cheesecake I planned to put on the menu, she acted put off.

Lauren had made quite an impact since arriving in town a year before me. She was equal parts savvy entrepreneur and lightning rod for controversy. Her genius cheese-maker, Ethan, and exotic cheeses had captivated the foodie crowd, but her frosty attitude and business tactics had alienated many locals. As I watched Lauren bark orders at Ethan and Sophia, I pondered whether she'd ever soften up or possibly even switch out of her Armani suits for something a little more casual.

"Looks like a fun morning at Cheese Headquarters," I muttered, filling a paper cup with a latte. The rich aroma of coffee mingled with mint and vanilla wafted up, momentarily distracting me from the Lauren Yancey Show.

As the morning progressed, the lake's shoreline came alive. More vendors arrived, setting up colorful pop-up canopies that dotted the landscape. Artists began to chisel blocks of ice into what would transform into dazzling sculptures while the crisp air vibrated with the warm, infectious chatter distinct to our small-town festivals.

"Parker!" a familiar voice called out.

Hazel—my tech-whiz, true-crime-obsessed baking prodigy of a college student cafe assistant—bounded toward me, her pastel mint-colored hair a festive beacon in the morning frost. And yes, once again, she had changed her hair color, this time to coordinate with our new mint latte. Her infectious energy was staggering—how could anyone be so relentlessly chipper, regardless of time, place or temperature?

"Morning, Hazel," I said, handing her a cup of the Minted Mayhem. "Careful, it's hot. Unlike, you know, everything else around here."

Hazel took a sip and let out a contented sigh. "Oh, this is perfect. We're going to be the most popular booth at the Frost Fest!"

"Great. I've always wanted to be prom queen of the hypothermia ball." I winked.

"The Grinch called. He wants his attitude back," Hazel chided and elbowed me. "This is going to be amazing! Did you see the ice sculptures they're carving? And did you see the alpacas for the petting zoo!"

"Nothing says winter fun like petting large, spitting animals," I deadpanned. "Thanks for bringing the cheesecakes, by the way. Let's get them set up."

Hazel moved to help, carefully arranging sample-sized slices of her cheesecake on tiered platters. I had to admit, the girl had talent. Not only for making delicious sweet treats but also for turning the cafe's kitchen into an astonishing mess. Which I'd come to accept because she was, quite frankly, worth it. For the cheesecake, she had concocted a few different selections: chocolate, salted caramel and the traditional New York style. All three were deliciously scrumptious.

Just as we were putting the finishing touches on our display, a booming voice cut through the morning air. "Well, well! If it isn't Magnolia Grove's favorite caffeine dealer!"

I turned to see Walter Carr, a local dairy farmer up in years, approaching, his chest puffed out like an old but still proud rooster. The man swaggered like he owned the place, which, given how much of the town's dairy came from his farm, wasn't far from the truth.

What caught my attention was his outfit. Walter was bundled up top, wearing a thick coat and hat, but below the waist, he sported plaid swim trunks and woolen socks that reached up to his knees. He looked like a cross between a small-town farmer and a Scottish Highland athlete, ready to toss logs in the middle of Frost Fest.

"Morning, Walter. Coffee?" I offered him a cup.

"You bet your bottom dollar!" He took the coffee.

Hazel chimed in, "Ready for the big Polar Plunge contest, Walter?"

He let out a laugh that probably echoed to the next county. "Ready? Darlin', I was born ready. Twenty-five years running, and this year's gonna make it twenty-six. Ain't nobody can beat old Walter in that there Polar Plunge!"

Just then, a muscular, fit man with curly silver hair and a determined glint in his eye strode up. Despite the cold, he wore only a red velour tracksuit.

"Don't count your chickens before they hatch, Walter," the man said, his voice gruff but good-natured. "This might be the year I dethrone the king."

Walter guffawed. "George Baxter, you old coot! Still think you can beat me? Second place twenty-five years running ain't no small feat, but first place? That's my territory!"

George's chocolate-brown eyes narrowed, but a smile played at the corners of his mouth. "We'll see about that. I've been training in my shower all year long. You better watch your back, old man."

"The only thing I'll be watching is you shivering in my wake, George!" Walter called out as George walked away, shaking his head and laughing.

I bit back a snarky comment about brave (or crazy) souls diving into the freezing lake. "Well, good luck out there."

"Luck! Don't need it. Got ice water in my veins, I do." Walter sipped his coffee, then glanced over at Lauren Yancey's booth and spoke loudly. "Say, you think Ms.

Lauren over there might step up to the Polar Plunge? Show us locals how it's done?"

Lauren, overhearing, scoffed loudly. "Please. I'd sooner dive into a vat of spoiled milk than participate in that display of frostbite-inducing flexing. And by the way, don't think I haven't forgotten about how you 'accidentally' gave me buffalo milk instead of goat milk. Ruined an entire batch of chèvre."

Walter's face reddened. "Consider it payback for unhitching Bessie's gate!"

I well remembered that day a few weeks back. I'd been wiping down tables at Catch You Latte when Bessie, Walter's prized Holstein, came marching down Main Street as though she belonged there. The sight of a 1,500-pound cow sauntering past my window, stopping traffic and causing general chaos, wasn't something you forget easily.

Lauren's eyes narrowed. "I have no idea what you're talking about, Walter. Maybe if you spent less time accusing others and more time securing your livestock, you wouldn't have cows running amok in town."

Walter waved her off and wandered away, grumbling aloud over his shoulder, "You'll get your comeuppance, city slicker."

I shook my head, wondering if this dairy farmer-versus-artisanal cheese-maker feud would ever resolve.

Hazel bit her lip. "Those two have really got it out for one another, huh?"

Before I could reply, there was a sudden sharp crack

that echoed from the distance. Lauren ducked instinctively, and I nearly upended an entire table.

"What the heck was that?" I asked, heart pounding. "Gunshots?"

Whit appeared at my elbow, looking annoyingly unruffled. "Don't worry," he said, his voice calm. "It's just the Hodgson brothers. Their property over yonder backs up to the lake, and they use weekends for target practice."

I stared at him, wondering if I'd wandered into some kind of rustic twilight zone. "And nobody thought to, I don't know, ask them to hold off during a public event?"

Whit shrugged. "Welcome to small-town life, Parker. Where your neighbor's hobby might just give you a heart attack, but at least they'll bring you some cornbread afterward."

I shook my head, marveling at the beautiful absurdity of it all. If someone had told me a year ago that I'd be standing by a frozen lake, slinging coffee and listening to gunshots in the morning, I'd have asked if they'd lost their mind!

Another incident from Lauren's booth caught my attention. Ethan and Sophia were huddled together, whispering frantically, as Sophia was trying to shove a rolled-up canvas back into a cardboard tube.

"Now what's going on over there?" Hazel wondered aloud.

Ethan took the tube from Sophia. "Let me see it." He removed the canvas and unrolled it on the ground, his eyes going wide. He quickly rolled it back up, shooting a panicked look at Sophia.

"Told you it was bad," Sophia shot back.

Lauren, who'd been busy walking cheese boards to and from her car, took note of her employees fussing about. "Sophia! Where's our banner? It needs to be up front and center!"

Ethan and Sophia looked like two deer in headlights.

"Um, about that," Sophia began, her voice trying to find confidence. "Seems like there was a ... misprint at the sign place."

Lauren's eyes narrowed. "Figures. Well, let me see. How bad could it be?"

Ethan, looking like he'd rather be anywhere else, reluctantly unrolled the banner.

Over the "Feta & Friends" logo, red spray paint spelled out: "FETA & FIENDS: GREEDY CITY SLICKER GO HOME!"

"That's not a misprint! What is the meaning of this?!" Lauren shrieked, nearly dropping the cheese display she held.

Ethan stood frozen, his mouth hanging open. Sophia looked ready to bolt.

"What happened here?" Lauren demanded, her eyes sweeping over her mortified employees. "I want to know who's responsible for this ... this act of vandalism!"

Sophia mumbled, "I don't know."

"You don't know? This was in your possession!"

"This is the first time I'm taking it out of the container. I have no idea what happened!" Sophia said.

"Well, you better figure this out!" Lauren said. "And I want my money back."

Sophia grabbed her tablet and began typing away. "I'm working on it. But, you know … maybe Parker can help? She's good at solving mysteries."

I ducked behind the table. Nope. Not how I was going to spend my day, or any other day for that matter.

Lauren's lips pressed into a thin line. "I don't need a coffee-pouring armchair sleuth poking around my business. You figure it out, Sophia. But I'm pretty sure I know who did this. He's going to pay—" She cut herself off, taking a deep breath. When she spoke again, her voice was low and dangerous. "Someone's trying to ruin me. Well, they picked the wrong lady to mess with."

Out of the corner of my eye, I spotted Walter Carr watching the scene unfold. His weathered face bore an expression I can only describe as amused satisfaction. He stood there, arms crossed, a slight smirk playing at the corners of his mouth. It reminded me of an artist admiring their handiwork.

Sophia's eyes darted between Walter and Lauren, her head tilted slightly as if cataloging their reactions. "People are so predictable when they're angry," she said.

"Predictable?" Lauren asked, rearranging the cheese samples into perfect concentric circles.

"Oh, I just mean that emotions can be so … revealing."

"Enough of your psycho-babble. Just finish setting up this booth."

Something told me this Frost Fest was going to be anything but chill. And here I thought the most exciting thing today would be watching people willingly jump into a frozen lake. But as you can see, Magnolia Grove had other plans.

CHAPTER 2

The Frost Fest bustled as the locals began to arrive and stroll from booth to booth, sampling wares and making purchases. From behind my coffee stand, I surveyed the scene with a mix of amusement and affection. Laughter and chatter filled the air, punctuated by the rhythmic scraping of ice chisels transforming frozen blocks into glistening sculptures. The Ice Pickers, a local electric bluegrass band, plucked delightful tunes. In the distance, alpacas from the petting zoo bleated, their fuzzy heads poking over the fence as children giggled and offered them treats.

Maggie Thomas—the owner of Boutique Chic—strolled up to the booth. Her cheeks were rosy from the cold, and her wild red curls spilled out from under her white-knit cap. "I'll take one of those Minted Mayhem Lattes. Hopefully, it'll keep me from turning into a human popsicle in the Polar Plunge."

I stopped mid-pour. "You're jumping into that icy lake?"

"I do every year."

"I'm impressed, Maggie. You continue to amaze me ... your latte is coming right up."

A moment later, I handed Maggie the steaming cup.

She smiled and sipped the drink. "And you continue to impress me, Parker. You know, you played a role in my spiritual transformation."

"Me? Spiritual?"

"You never judged me. Just helped me question some of my more unsavory decisions for what they were."

She was referencing the affair she'd had with the former mayor.

"Well, I'm glad I was able to talk some sense into you," I joked.

"That's right. And then God did the rest. Well, I better get back to my booth. I hope you have a blessed day today, Parker!" She waved goodbye.

The reformed Maggie Thomas was a breath of fresh air, and I was thankful for her friendship.

Hazel bounced over, her mint-colored hair bobbing with each step. "Parker, you've got to see the ice sculpture of Major! It looks just like him, right down to the little bowtie!"

I raised an eyebrow. "I bet it's adorable."

Major, Clyde's loyal companion, had taken on a dual role: my sometimes weekend dog and trusted sounding board. Clyde, my go-to handyman and renovation genius, who had transformed my crumbling building into a charming cafe and cozy upstairs apartment, would often stroke his puffy white beard and chuckle, "Seems Major's adopted you, Parker!"

My gaze drifted over the festival grounds. The vendor booths were a kaleidoscope of color against the stark white snow. The scent of cinnamon and warm sugar wafted from the Ambling sisters' booth, where they were making many friends with their fried dough. Even Lauren Yancey's cheese display looked festive despite her earlier meltdown over the vandalized banner.

A squeal of microphone feedback made everyone within a fifty-foot radius wince and look at the stage. Nellie Pritchett's voice, amplified to near-painful levels, boomed across the festival grounds. "Testing … is it on?" Nellie, Magnolia Grove's mayor pro tem and official know-it-all, resplendent in a puffy white coat that made her look like an overgrown marshmallow, was attempting to wrangle the microphone into submission.

She tapped the mic again, then spoke. "Welcome, one and all, to Magnolia Grove's annual Frost Fest!"

People began to congregate near the stage.

I leaned toward Hazel and Whit. "Ten bucks says she mentions 'cozy cold weather carnival' at least twice."

"Fool's bet." Whit smiled.

Hazel giggled. "You're on."

Nellie's enthusiasm cranked up to eleven. "We've got a day chock-full of frosty fun ahead of us! From our ice sculpture contest to the highly anticipated Polar Plunge, this cozy cold weather carnival has something for everyone!"

I held out my hand to Hazel, wiggling my fingers. "Pay up, buttercup."

"She's only said it once," Hazel protested.

"Just wait for it …"

Sure enough, Nellie's voice rang out again. "So, bundle up, grab some hot coffee from Parker there, go take some pictures with the alpacas and enjoy all the other delights our little cozy cold weather carnival has to offer!"

Hazel sighed, slapping a ten-dollar bill into my palm. "You know her too well."

I tucked the money away with a smirk. "It's a gift and a curse."

Just then, a minor commotion ensued. A disheveled man with a scruffy beard and a tattered baseball cap over his messy mullet stumbled onto the platform. His eyes were glassy, his movements uncoordinated. The festive crowd fell silent as he swayed dangerously close to the edge of the stage.

"Who's that?" I asked.

Whit shook his head. "That's Jesse Carr. Walter's son and the town's most reliable troublemaker. Been a bit more unhinged lately."

"He looks drunk," Hazel noted.

Whit quickly headed toward the stage.

Great. Nothing says "family-friendly festival" like a drunk guy hijacking the mic. At ten o'clock in the morning, no less.

"Hey, I wanna say somethin'," Jesse slurred, yanking the microphone from a startled Nellie.

I groaned. "This ought to be good."

Jesse swayed slightly, gripping the mic stand for balance. "I'd like to thank this lovely town," he drawled, sarcasm dripping from every word, "for lookin' the other way while city slickers like Lauren Yancey take over our businesses."

Lauren's head snapped up at the mention of her name, her eyes glaring.

"Looks like Jesse has some grievances to air," I muttered.

Jesse continued, his voice rising, "And a special thanks to my dear old pops, the Polar Plunge king himself, for decidin' to sell our family farm—my rightful inheritance, thank you very much ... And how about a special shoutout to that turncoat Ronald Sweetwater for stealin' right out from under me!" He pointed vaguely at no one in the crowd. "Where'd you go, Ronald?" Jesse squinted, leering at the crowd, looking for Ronald, who seemed to be absent. The crowd shifted uncomfortably. Nellie frantically motioned to Whit offstage, her plastered-on smile slipping.

Within seconds, Whit gently but firmly escorted a still-ranting Jesse off the stage. Nellie quickly reclaimed the microphone, her voice overly bright as she tried to salvage the situation.

"Well, folks, how about we get this Frost Fest truly started? Don't forget to visit all our wonderful vendors! Oh, and—heads up, Polar Plunge daredevils—meet down at the dock at 1:55 PM! We're dunking you brave souls at two o'clock sharp!"

With that, the Ice Pickers resumed their spots and the music kicked into high gear.

As the folks began to meander about, I caught Whit's eye as he passed, leading a now-sullen Jesse away. He gave me a resigned shrug.

A line of people began to form at my booth. Hazel and I got to work, moving in perfect sync like a well-oiled machine, distributing coffee drinks and slices of cheese-cake. She'd pull espresso shots while I'd steam milk, our movements choreographed with the precision of a dance routine.

Clyde, bundled up against the cold, stepped up to the booth with Major by his side. The little black-and-white dog sported an adorable baby blue sweater which made me smile. I gave Clyde a cup of his usual dark roast and a slice of chocolate cheesecake, then tossed a dog treat to Major. I always carried a few in my pocket for my little buddy.

Nellie Pritchett bustled up to the booth, her cheeks flushed with excitement. "Oh, Parker, despite that little mishap with Jesse Carr, isn't this just the most delightful event? The community spirit is simply overflowing!"

"Yes, it is, Nellie. Coffee?"

Just as I reached for a paper cup, the space heater died. The espresso machine sputtered to a halt mid-brew.

I called over to the Feta & Friends booth, "Do you all have power still?"

Ethan gave a thumbs-up.

"Ugh. I'll go check the generator," I said. "Hazel, hold down the fort."

I left our booth and walked toward the main generator. "Oh, the joys of outdoor winter festivals."

When I reached the gas generator, a teenager with

shaggy hair and a denim jacket with patches stood next to the large piece of machinery, holding a few cables in his hand and looking discombobulated.

"Hey, I think you unplugged me," I said.

"Sorry, ma'am. The band asked me to run the soundboard, and I honestly don't know much about this stuff."

"Here, let me help ..."

I bent down and plugged the cord back into the generator.

On my way back to my booth, I heard what sounded like an intense conversation coming from the other side of the trees. Of course, I stopped to listen. I couldn't help myself.

"Why do you have to be so hostile, Lauren? The locals are your bread and butter." The voice was calm and measured, and I didn't recognize it. But someone was reprimanding Lauren Yancey. My interest sparked. I inched closer.

"Hostile?! This is business, Jules. Why does everyone have to be so sensitive," Lauren snapped.

"Well, Walter Carr terminated the deal."

"How is that my fault?"

"Once he learned you're one of my business partners, he pulled out."

"Okay ... How is that my problem? That has nothing to do with Feta & Friends."

"Well, Lauren, it just so happens all of my portfolios are integrated. I was depending on this venture to bring in a windfall."

Deciding I'd eavesdropped on these two businesswomen enough, I began to sneak away but slipped on a patch of ice, landing on my backside.

Lauren peered out from behind the cluster of trees, her eyes slicing into me. Without a word, she stalked off.

I stood up, brushing snow off of me.

A woman—Jules, I assumed—approached, exuding confidence and poise. Her sleek black hair cascaded in elegant waves, complemented by her luxurious gray wool coat, double-breasted and impeccably tailored. Her gaze was piercing yet pleasant, scrutinizing me with shrewd intelligence.

"Are you okay?" she asked, her voice tinged with a refined Southern accent.

"Oh, I'm fine. Slipping and falling keeps me limber."

"You wouldn't happen to be Parker Hayes, by chance?"

"Guilty as charged."

She extended a manicured hand. "I've heard about you. I'm Jules Winston."

I shook her hand. "Nice to meet you. I'd love to chat, but I've got a caffeine-deprived mob to appease."

"Mind if I walk with you?"

"Not at all."

Jules fell into step beside me as I headed back to my booth.

"What brings you to our humble little town, Jules?"

"Grew up here. Still have my cabin over on the other side of the lake. I'll mosey up from Charlotte for a few weeks now and then. Check up on some of my local partnerships."

"Like Feta & Friends. Sounds *real* chummy ... Sorry, I couldn't help overhearing."

Jules waved the air. "Ah, yes. Lauren Yancey can be abrasive," she said, her voice smooth as butter. "She's just a bit stressed about the business and all this festival stuff. She's still ... getting accustomed to a slower pace of life."

"It's been over a year," I blurted.

Jules laughed, a practiced sound that probably worked wonders in boardrooms. "You're funny, Parker. And talented, too, from what I understand. I must try this coffee of yours that's been getting rave reviews."

"Thanks. I do my best to keep Magnolia Grove marginally less tired and groggy."

"Out of curiosity: Have you ever considered expanding?"

My intrigue flickered to life, but before I could respond, we reached my booth. A line of impatient customers had formed. Hazel was doing her best to hand out drinks and slices of cheesecake.

"Duty calls," I said, stepping behind the table.

Hazel's eyes went wide as saucers when she spotted Jules. She tugged on my sleeve, practically vibrating with excitement.

"Parker, that's Jules Winston! She's, like, a business legend!"

I smirked, amused by Hazel's customary starstruck behavior. "Okay, fan girl."

Jules leaned on the table, seemingly unfazed by Hazel's gushing. "I'd love to chat more about the future of your coffee, Parker. We'll talk later."

"Sure," I said, only half listening as I prepared three Minted Mayhem Lattes simultaneously.

As Jules strolled away, Hazel clutched my arm. "Jules Winston helped turn a failing smoothie shop in Charlotte into a multi-million-dollar empire! Got her hand in all sorts of business and housing developments. She also knows how to fly a plane! She's like a big shot!"

"Wow, how do you know so much about her?"

Hazel grinned. "Doing my final essay on her for my business class. She's kind of one of my heroes. Next to you, of course."

I focused on serving hot drinks to the cold people, wondering why on earth a successful entrepreneur pilot like Jules Winston wanted to talk about my little coffee shop. Especially since she hadn't even tried the coffee.

THE AFTERNOON SUN did its feeble best to warm the chilly air. Things at the booth had slowed down. Hazel and I were able to relax next to the space heater and enjoy some cheesecake. I had the salted caramel, which melted in my mouth in a swirl of sugary saltiness that made me forget about the cold weather. Right as I took my last bite, the space heater died along with the coffee equipment.

"Not again," I groaned.

"I'll go plug it back in this time," Hazel said, rushing off.

In the distance, a single pop of gunfire signaled that the Hodgson brothers had resumed their target practice over on their property.

Hazel returned, although the power hadn't come back on.

"What's wrong?" I asked.

"Generator ran out of gas. Clyde's filling it back up."

While we waited, the festival continued like nothing had happened. Ice sculptures glittered in the sunlight, their crystalline forms showcasing remarkable skill. The bluegrass band played an unplugged acoustic tune while a few locals danced in front of the stage. Distant squeals from kids pierced the air. One of the alpacas—most likely tired of being yanked at by children all day—made a break for freedom. The furry creature sauntered right up to my booth like it wanted to order a cup of coffee.

"Well, hello there," I said to my unexpected customer.

I pulled out my phone to capture the moment. Right when I pressed the button, a giant pink tongue slurped across my screen. The resulting photo showed a close-up of alpaca tastebuds, though you could spot those gentle brown eyes in the corner of the frame. Dad would get a kick out of this one—an endless supply of animal puns would undoubtedly ensue.

A guy in his mid-twenties with flushed cheeks dashed over and grabbed the lead rope dangling from the animal's halter. "Sorry about that, ma'am." He tugged gently on the rope. "Come on, Pumpkin." They walked away.

Whit bumped my elbow. "I'd say she liked you, Parker."

"Yeah, well, Pumpkin and I will always have this moment." I wiped the alpaca saliva off my phone with my sleeve and checked the time. "It's almost 1:55, Whit. You know what that means—time for the Polar Plunge."

Whit began to bounce on his toes like a boxer before a match. "I better get down there ..."

"You're really doing it, huh? I think I saw chunks of ice floating in the lake ..."

"You know me, I'm all about tradition." He gave me a heartwarming smile and a wink.

"Traditionally nuts."

"You sure you don't want to give it a try?"

"Oh, I'm sure."

"Come on, it's for charity."

"There are warmer ways to be charitable."

Whit pulled me close and gave me a kiss, which warmed my lips and made me want to call it a day.

"Well, I better head down yonder," he said with a dreamy grin.

I waved off Whit. "Don't freeze to death!"

I figured I'd start cleaning up the booth. I gathered empty cups and plates scattered around the table. On my way to the trash bin, I came upon Jesse Carr. He stood in the pathway near our booth, swaying a little.

"You okay, Jesse?" I asked.

He grunted something incoherent and then staggered off.

In the distance, the generator rumbled to life, and the power came back on.

The band stopped playing, and Nellie's voice crackled over the loudspeaker.

"Attention, Frost Fest attendees! A few announcements ... Sorry about the inconvenience of our little power outage; looks like we got the generator refueled. Thanks,

Clyde! ... And everyone will be glad to know Pumpkin is safely back in her pen. Also, it appears someone has run into our beloved statue of Magnolia Grove's town founder. It has toppled over, blocking the exit. Rest assured, a crew is working on it and should have it cleared shortly. And now, the moment you've all been waiting for is almost here! Our brave Polar Plunge participants are gathering by the lake. Meet us down by the dock. Don't forget, it's for charity! The one with the longest time will be crowned champion! And if you beat Water Carr's record of seven minutes and forty-nine seconds, you win a dinner for two at The Old Courthouse Grill."

Everyone began to walk down toward the dock. The gathering crowd was a mix of excited spectators, a couple of wetsuit-wearing emergency personnel and participants who looked like they might be reconsidering their life choices. Jackson Beauregard stood out amidst the crowd, radiating effortless confidence in his swim trunks and robe. Our history flashed through my mind—the dilapidated building his company sold me, his brother's murder, and his ambiguously flirtatious hints. Jackson's influence remained strong in Magnolia Grove, wielded with surgical precision and refined old-money charm. Whit caught my eye and waved, his smile a bit strained. I'd tried to talk him out of this madness, but apparently, "town historian" also meant "guy who jumps into frozen lakes for charity."

George Baxter, Walter's Polar Plunge arch-rival, was doing calisthenics and breathing exercises, his fit frame a testament to his competitive spirit. Maggie Thomas, her signature red locks hidden beneath a stylish floral swim cap, chatted with cheese-maker Ethan Fontaine, who, though he was not plunging, looked to be giving her words of encouragement. Surprisingly, the retired archeology professor, Dr. Rufus Delacroix, hurried past in his swimsuit, explaining to Pastor Jasper the therapeutic benefits of cold-water immersion. The middle-aged pastor looked pale but resolute.

Hazel nudged me. "Look who just joined them! I can't believe Jules is doing it too!" She pointed to the bath-robed businesswoman walking up to the dock.

I scanned the gathering crowd. Something was off.

"Hey, where's Walter Carr? Shouldn't the reigning Polar Plunge champion be front and center for this?"

Hazel frowned, standing on tiptoe to get a better view. "You're right. I don't see him anywhere."

I remembered Walter's boasting earlier that morning. He seemed to be born ready for his twenty-sixth consecutive plunge. So where was he?

"Maybe he chickened out?" Hazel suggested.

I shook my head. "Not likely. He wouldn't miss this for the world."

"Maybe a dramatic entrance?" Hazel suggested.

The contestants began lining up on the dock, but Walter still hadn't arrived. Something felt more and more wrong. The murmur of the crowd grew louder as people began to notice Walter's absence. I overheard snippets of conversation, worry creeping into voices usually filled with small-town cheer.

"Where's old Walter?"

"Didn't he say something about making it twenty-six years?"

"Maybe he's just running late?"

I exchanged a glance with Hazel. "I've got a bad feeling about this."

Nellie's voice crackled over the loudspeaker again, her usual pep sounding forced. "Paging Walter Carr ... paging Walter Carr. It seems we're missing our reigning Polar Plunge champion. Has anyone seen Walter?"

The festival grounds erupted into a flurry of activity. People began calling out Walter's name, peering behind booths and trees as if the dairy farmer might be hiding behind a snow-covered shrub. A feeling of unease grew in my gut.

I made my way closer to the lake, my eyes scanning the shoreline. The icy water lapped at the edges, deceptively peaceful.

A commotion near a small inlet caught my attention. My heart sank as I saw a group of people gathered at the water's edge, pointing at something floating in the distance.

"No," I muttered, picking up my pace. "Please, no."

I pushed through the crowd, my breath catching in my throat as I saw what had captured everyone's attention.

There, bobbing gently in the frigid water, was a body.

CHAPTER 3

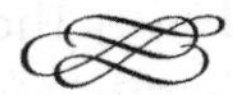

The icy water lapped at the two EMTs' wetsuits as they pulled the body out of the lake and onto the bluff. The garish plaid swim trunks, a jarring splash of color against the gray lake and somber pine surroundings, confirmed it was Walter Carr. We stood in a small, secluded cove surrounded by towering pine trees, their evergreen branches swaying gently in the chilly air.

"Well, the reigning Polar Plunge champion won't be defending his title this year," I said, taking in the scene.

Whit's face fell. "Terrible. Poor Walter." He glanced out at the lake before meeting my gaze. "No Polar Plunge this year, I suppose. I'm going to go change."

The other contestants—Jules, Maggie, Dr. Rufus Delacroix, Pastor Jasper and Jackson—followed behind Whit. Only George remained, his eyes fixed on the body of his longtime rival, Walter.

"Parker!" Hazel's voice cut through my concentration. "Did he drown?"

"Not sure."

I turned to face the growing crowd of onlookers surrounding us. Their faces wore shock, fascination and that particular brand of small-town concern that's equal parts genuine worry and eagerness for gossip. Nellie, hands on hips, looked like she was trying to make sense of the whole thing. This was supposed to be a simple winter festival. Hot lattes, ice sculptures, bluegrass, alpacas and the entertaining spectacle of my neighbors willingly jumping into a frozen lake. Now I was standing over a dead body, my amateur sleuth senses tingling like they'd been dunked in my strongest espresso.

One of the EMTs carefully turned over Walter's body. My breath caught as I spotted a small, dark hole in Walter's chest.

"No, Hazel," I said. "This was no accidental drowning."

A series of sharp cracks echoed from a distance, making several onlookers jump. The Hodgson brothers and their target practice.

Deputy Colton loped down the slope with long strides, his lanky frame exhibiting surprising agility for a man of his years.

He stroked his silver push-broom mustache. "Is that ...?"

One of the EMTs nodded. "Looks like he's been shot."

Colton's eyes widened as he processed the words, his gaze dropping to the wound in Walter's chest. Another volley of gunshots rang out, making him flinch.

"Dagnabbit," he muttered, then turned to his deputy. "Granger! Get someone to mosey on over to the Hodgson place and tell 'em to cool their heels on that firing range. Last thing we need is folks thinkin' we're under attack." He scanned the immediate area and shook his head when he saw all the footsteps that had already populated the snow in the crime scene. "Call in forensics. Back these people away and grab the yellow tape from your cruiser. We got a bonafide shooting."

Granger—a stocky man with a face like a bulldog—nodded and started telling people to back away before he lumbered off to get the crime scene tape.

Colton turned to the EMTs. "Not much y'all can do for him now. I think we'll leave the body as-is until forensics shows up. Cool your heels until then. Thanks." They nodded and withdrew from the immediate scene.

Colton's gaze swept across the lake, then locked onto mine. With a subtle nod, he drew me aside, creating some distance between us and the curious onlookers. His expression was tense.

"Listen, Parker, Sheriff Sinclair's out of town. Some law enforcement conference in Raleigh. I'm ... I'm not going to lie. I wouldn't be troubled if you offered a bit of a hand here with this incident. I ain't no homicide detective."

I raised an eyebrow. "I'm flattered. But need I remind you, Deputy, that I run a coffee shop, not a detective agency?"

He shifted uncomfortably. His kind gray eyes pleaded. "Yeah, but you've got special savvy with this sort of thing. And let's face it, you've solved more murders in this town than ... well, than there should be murders in a town this size. If this is a murder and not some stray bullet from those yay-hoos over yonder."

I sighed, knowing he had a point. Magnolia Grove did seem to have an unusually high body count for a place whose motto is "Where Our People Are as Sweet as Our Blossoms."

Who was I kidding? I could make a million resolutions, change my identity and move to the moon, and I'd still end up knee-deep in a murder investigation. Maybe it was time to face facts: trouble followed me like Major followed the scent of dog treats. Might as well embrace my apparent destiny as Magnolia Grove's resident amateur sleuth, eh?

I tucked a strand of hair behind my ear. "How about a solid 'maybe'... But let's get one thing straight—if I assist, I'm not *officially* involved. I'm just a concerned citizen who happens to make a mean latte and have an inconvenient knack for solving crimes."

Colton nodded eagerly. "Of course, of course. Just ... keep your eyes open, will you?"

"Alright, Deputy," I said. "I'll do what I can. But don't expect miracles. And for the love of all that's caffeinated, please keep this quiet. The last thing I need is for the whole town to think I'm some kind of small-town Sherlock."

Colton chuckled. "They already do."

I suppose some things couldn't be helped.

I scanned the crowd, taking mental notes of everyone's reactions. I paid particular attention to Lauren Yancey, who was pacing back and forth behind the crowd, phone pressed to her ear.

Granger returned with the yellow crime scene tape and started cordoning off the scene.

Colton's hands were shaking. "Parker. I don't suppose you've got any coffee left in that booth of yours? I've got a feeling it's gonna be a long one."

"Come on, let's get you some of my special 'Oh-Great-There's-Been-A-Murder' blend. Extra strong with a hint of 'why-did-I-agree-to-this' flavor."

He managed a weak chuckle. "You're a lifesaver, Parker."

As I turned to leave, I noticed something glinting in the snow near the towering pine. Instinctively, I moved closer, my eyes narrowing as I tried to make out what it was.

"Hey, Colton," I called out, gesturing to the spot. "You might want to take a look over here. I think I spotted something interesting."

Colton hurried over. He crouched down, examining the area closely with a furrowed brow. "Well, I'll be," he muttered. "It's a shell casing. And judging by the size, we're talking about a pistol, not a rifle. 9mm."

He stood up, shaking his head. "This rules out any chance it was an accidental shooting from them Hodgson boys. We've got ourselves a bonafide murder on our hands."

I nodded grimly, surveying the scene. Though the location was relatively near the booths, it was in a secluded inlet and surrounded by trees. It was the perfect spot for the crime. My initial observations revealed:

•Besides the tracks on the path leading into and out of

the alcove, there weren't other tracks leading away from the scene, indicating the killer returned to the festival.

•The killer cleverly used the Hodgson brothers' target shooting as cover for the gunshot. The first shot I'd heard when they resumed their shooting was somewhere around 1:45 PM, from what I recalled.

•The fact that the parking lot's exit had been blocked by the fallen statue of the town's founder at what I estimated was the time of the shooting suggested the killer must've blended in with the crowd.

"Deputy, I recommend questioning festival-goers about their whereabouts between 1:30 and 2 PM. Ask if they saw anything suspicious around that time, especially near this area. And don't let anyone leave."

The deputy nodded. "Will do, Parker. Appreciate your insight."

I started to head back toward my booth, Colton by my side. Whit—back in his jeans and flannel—intercepted us halfway up the slope, his face etched with concern. "Parker, please tell me you're not getting mixed up in this."

I gave him a wry smile. "Whit, you know me by now."

He sighed, a mix of exasperation and fondness in his eyes. "Here we go again."

Before I could respond, Jesse Carr came barreling down the path toward us.

"What's this I'm hearing about my pop? He's been shot?!" he bellowed.

Colton moved quickly to intercept him. "Now, son, we're handling this. I'm gonna need you to settle down. Can you do that for me?"

Jesse's face cycled through a kaleidoscope of emotions —grief, rage, confusion. Then he turned back around, his gaze locked onto Lauren Yancey, who had returned to her booth.

"You!" he snarled, jabbing a finger in her direction. "You did this, you city-slicking, cheese-pushing …" The rest of his words dissolved into an incoherent string of curses and accusations.

Colton grabbed hold of Jesse, trying to calm him down. A few more deputies arrived on the scene, finally giving Colton some much-needed backup.

"Deputies," Colton called out, "start taking down names and contact information. Nobody leaves without checking in first."

I watched as Colton fumbled with his radio, requesting the status of his forensics unit. His face was pale, forehead beaded with sweat despite the cold air. Poor guy looked about as comfortable as a long-tailed cat in a room full of rocking chairs.

Colton pointed at a young, wide-eyed deputy and another who looked fresh out of the Marines. "Nia, get statements from anyone who might've seen anything. Travis, handle Jesse. Ensure no one leaves."

Jesse blurted, "This is bull—" but Travis swiftly silenced him, clamping a meaty hand on his shoulder.

"Easy there, Jesse," Travis rumbled calmly. "Let's have a word, shall we?"

Travis and a somewhat subdued Jesse walked over to the side of the stage.

As the deputies scrambled to contain the situation, the

barely concealed panic in Colton's eyes was obvious. He was in way over his head, and he knew it.

Nellie marched over, her face a mix of concern and barely disguised excitement. "Oh my stars, Deputy Colton! What a to-do! Is there anything I can do to help? Perhaps make an announcement?"

Colton looked like he was about to refuse, then thought better of it. "Actually, Ms. Pritchett, that might be helpful. If you could ask everyone to remain calm and cooperate with the deputies, that'd be great."

Nellie beamed, practically sashaying to the stage.

Her voice boomed over the loudspeaker, somehow both soothing and nerve-inducing at the same time. "Ladies and gentlemen of Magnolia Grove, if I could have your attention, please. In light of this afternoon's tragic event, we ask that everyone remain calm and—"

"You killed him!" Jesse's voice cut through her announcement. He broke free from Travis, stumbling toward Lauren's booth. "You stuck-up city slicker!"

Lauren stepped back with her hands raised. "Jesse, please—"

He lurched into the display table, sending wheels of cheese tumbling. Lauren's designer handbag flew off the table, its contents scattering across the snow. Something metallic glinted in the winter sun.

The crowd fell silent.

A collective gasp rippled through the onlookers. Ethan scrambled to pick up the fallen cheese samples while Sophia stood frozen behind the booth, her face a perfect mask of shock. Lauren's complexion matched the snow at her feet as she stared at the gun lying exposed among her scattered belongings. It was a Glock 9mm.

"Well," Jesse slurred, swaying slightly. "Looks like someone came prepared."

Colton's eyes narrowed with determination as he strode toward the booth. Lauren backed away, shaking her head. "That's not … I didn't …"

I caught Whit's eye. He raised an eyebrow, and I shrugged in response.

Looked like I wouldn't be needed after all. But I was still a bit stunned. Could I have seen Lauren sabotaging the inside of Walter's swimsuit with Ben-Gay? Yes. But shooting him and dumping his body in the lake?

That was a whole different story.

Didn't see that coming.

CHAPTER 4

Catch You Latte's doorbell rang out, welcoming another patron to our cozy haven, now the epicenter of Magnolia Grove's murder intrigue. Since Saturday's shocking events, Walter Carr's name had been on everyone's lips, sparking fervent whispers and theories that refused to fade by Tuesday.

I wiped down the counter for what felt like the thousandth time that morning, my ears perking up at snippets of chatter floating around the room.

"I heard he was shot with an antique revolver, bless his heart." Mrs. Pumpling spoke in a low voice to her garden club friends.

I bit back a grin. The woman couldn't keep a geranium alive, but she'd suddenly become an expert on firearms?

"Well, I understand Lauren Yancey and Walter were romantically involved," her companion replied, voice dripping with scandal.

My snort of laughter was masked by the hiss of the

espresso machine. These people had been watching too many soap operas. Lauren Yancey and Walter Carr? That was about as likely as me winning the Nobel Peace Prize.

The aroma of Hazel's mint-chocolate cheesecake wafted through the air just moments before she appeared from the kitchen carrying the freshly baked dessert.

"You know," I muttered to her as she passed, "with all this interest in Walter's case, maybe we should start an open mic night: 'Theories and Treats Tuesdays'!"

Hazel giggled, carefully placing the cheesecake into the display case. "That's not a bad idea. I bet we'd have quite the turnout."

"Maybe we could even have a 'guess the ending' contest," I said, eyeing the growing line of customers.

"Yeah, the winner gets free coffee for a week!"

"I was joking, Hazel."

She rolled her eyes and vanished back into the kitchen, where she would undoubtedly create another scrumptious masterpiece as well as another mess. I'd long surrendered to the chaos that accompanied her baking creativity—utensils scattered, flour dusting every surface and butter coating the countertops. It was the price of her genius. With a deep breath, I donned my warmest smile and greeted the next curious customer.

"Welcome to Catch You Latte," I chirped. "What can I get you today? We're serving up hot coffee with a side of wild suspicion."

The elderly man blinked at me, confused. "Uh, just a black coffee, please. Nothing on the side."

"You got it. One 'Just the Facts, Ma'am' coming right up. No frills, no thrills."

The cafe door jingled again, and in swept Nellie Pritchett, her honey-blonde hair swaying with each determined step. Several patrons nodded respectfully as she passed, murmuring "Morning, Mayor" under their breath.

I must say, after a few initial hiccups, Nellie had grown into her role as mayor pro tem. She'd taken to the job like a duck to water, balancing town business with her natural flair for … well, let's call it "community engagement" (though some might call it "gossip"). Part of me hoped she'd run for mayor in the special election come spring.

"Parker, honey," Nellie called out as she approached the counter. "I swear, I haven't had a moment's peace all morning. You wouldn't believe the hullabaloo down at the town hall!"

I tilted my head while measuring out Nellie's precise order—a vanilla latte with half-caf, quarter pump of sugar-free vanilla, a splash of oat milk, three ice cubes and my signature cinnamon smiley face dusting on top. "Let me guess, someone's protesting the new parking meters again?"

Nellie let out an exasperated sigh. "If only it were that simple. No, it's Ronald Sweetwater. He came storming into my office like a bull in a china shop."

Steam hissed from the espresso machine while I tamped down the grounds. "Ronald? The ice cream shop owner? The guy Jesse was yelling about at the festival? What's got his waffle cones in a twist?"

"He claims he has a right to Walter's dairy farm." Nellie

watched me carefully place three ice cubes into her drink before adding the precisely measured splash of oat milk. "Says Walter promised to sell it to him. Can you believe it? Ink's still wet on Walter's obituary and Ronald's already trying to stake his claim!"

I finished the drink with my trademark cinnamon smiley face and slid it across the counter. "Well, guess some folks have a PhD in opportunism."

Nellie took a long sip, closing her eyes in appreciation. "Mmm, Parker, perfect as always." She set the cup down. "And oh, it gets better. We tried explaining that just because he says he has the right to buy it, it doesn't mean anything. Not to be rude, but just taking his word holds no legal merit. But Ronald was having none of it. Stormed out of the town hall like a child who'd been denied his favorite candy."

"Yikes," I muttered, wiping down the steam wand.

Nellie looked around, then stage-whispered between sips of her latte, "Honestly, he seemed more upset about potentially losing his bid on the farm than about Walter being murdered. Isn't that something? He insisted there *is* a written contract. But if there is, nobody I know of has set eyeballs on it besides Walter and Ronald." She leaned in a little closer. "Oh, and get this: to add insult to Walter's injury … well, not like you can add injury to a man who's dead, but you know what I mean … a deputy driving back from the festival almost broadsided Bessie out on county route 2! Walter's cow had gotten out again, on the day Walter was murdered!"

"Unbelievable."

The bell chimed again. Maggie Thomas glided in, a vision of grace in her modest wool coat and boots. She'd traded her once-flamboyant style for something more in line with her new pious persona, but she still managed to make it look chic.

"Good morning, everyone," Maggie said, her voice syrupy sweet. "Isn't it just a beautiful day?"

I bit my tongue to keep from pointing out the gloomy, overcast sky outside while reaching for a mug. "Morning, Maggie. The usual?"

She shook her head. "I have grown quite fond of that new Minted Mayhem Latte. I'll have one of those, please."

I started preparing her drink. The rich aroma of freshly ground beans filled the air. Hazel popped out from the kitchen, this time with a fresh tray of her famous snicker-doodles in hand.

Maggie turned to Nellie. "Mayor Pritchett, I trust you're well? I've been praying for strength for your mayoral duties."

Nellie preened a bit at the "mayor" title, taking another sip of her perfectly crafted drink. "Why, thank you, Maggie. It's certainly been a challenge, what with poor Walter's murder and now all this hullabaloo about his farm."

I set Maggie's drink in front of her and piped up, "Speaking of hullabaloo, any news on Lauren? Last I heard, she was in a cell."

Maggie's eyes widened while she delicately tested her drink. "I don't think we really should gossip about such matters."

Nellie, however, was all too happy to spill the beans. "Well, since you asked, Lauren's out on bail. That slick attorney Roger Buzzard got her released."

So, good old Roger Buzzard was back in the picture …

Nellie continued. "Claimed she was an upstanding member of the community and posed no flight risk."

I snorted. "Lauren, upstanding? When did cold calculation, condescension and manipulation become the benchmarks of integrity?"

"Parker!" Maggie admonished.

Hazel, arranging her snickerdoodles, joined in. "Maybe she'll come storming in demanding her usual no-foam, extra-hot, definitely-not-county-jail latte with a side of alibi."

"Hazel!" Maggie gasped, nearly choking on her drink.

Nellie chuckled. "Well, I wouldn't put it past her. That woman's got more nerve than a bad tooth."

I shook my head. "Alright, as much as I enjoy a good Lauren roasting, maybe we should dial it back a notch. After all, she hasn't been convicted … yet."

Maggie chimed in sagely. "We must remember, judge not lest ye be judged. Lauren may have her … quirks, but she's still one of God's children."

"Yeah, the problem child who ate all the communion wafers and blamed it on the altar boy," I muttered.

Nellie cackled at that, nearly spitting out her drink. Even Maggie couldn't entirely hide her amusement, though she quickly covered it with a prim cough.

I leaned against the counter. "One thing that bothers

me: why wouldn't Lauren have simply tossed the gun into the lake? Why stash it in her purse?"

Hazel, ever my amateur sleuth protege, spoke up, "I think Lauren might not have been thinking clearly. She's not exactly a professional killer, you know?"

Nellie took a sip of her drink and then added, "Oh, yes. Or maybe she only meant to scare Walter, and things escalated. Accidentally shot him, then didn't know what to do, so she panicked and hid the gun."

I folded my arms. "Good points. But Lauren definitely looked stunned when the gun fell out of her purse. Although maybe she wasn't expecting Jesse to topple over her cheese display, causing the gun to fall out … I'm still unsure what to make of it."

The cafe door jingled once more, and a hush fell over the room as Jules Winston, business magnate and Hazel's personal hero, swept in. Her polished appearance radiated corporate power. She paused, taking in the scene with a friendly but shrewd gaze that seemed to assess everything and everyone in mere seconds.

Nellie, never one to miss an opportunity for insider information, piped up. "Jules! What perfect timing. We were just discussing the unfortunate business with Lauren Yancey. As her associate, what's your take on all this?"

I held my breath, curious despite myself. Jules's connection to Lauren as her primary investor was obvious, and I wondered how she'd handle this impromptu questioning.

Jules smiled, a polite yet guarded expression. "While I appreciate your interest, Mayor Pritchett, I make it a policy not to comment on ongoing legal matters. Innocent until proven guilty, after all."

Her diplomatic response impressed me. I'd half expected her to throw Lauren under the bus—or, should I say, into the cheese vat.

"However," Jules continued, smoothly changing the subject, "I would like to order something."

I could feel Hazel practically vibrating with excitement beside me. "Great. What can I get you?"

Jules scanned our menu board. "I'll try that Minted Mayhem Latte you mentioned at the fair. I've been thinking about it ever since."

"Good call. Hazel, would you do the honors?"

Hazel stood gobsmacked, staring at her business hero until I nudged her with my elbow.

"Oh, yeah. One Minted Mayhem. Coming right up!" She got to work like a little gerbil running on a wheel.

As Hazel prepared her drink, Jules glanced around the cafe. "I must say, Parker, you've created something special here. It's charming."

Maggie beamed. "Parker's been such a blessing to our little community."

Nellie nodded enthusiastically. "Absolutely! Parker's been a wonderful addition to Magnolia Grove. Her community spirit is as rich as her coffee blends."

Jules smiled. "I can tell. So, Parker, have you had a chance to think about my offer?"

I blinked, recalling our brief interaction at the festival. Jules had casually mentioned something about expansion. Since moving to Magnolia Grove, life had been a juggling act. Between navigating my own business, dodging murder accusations, assisting my parents in their preparation to move to town, and oh yeah, solving the occasional homicide, "expansion" hadn't exactly been at the top of my to-do list. Besides, I'd already had my brush with viral fame thanks to my former true-crime podcast, *Criminally Yours*. There was something comforting about keeping things small and cozy. I liked knowing my regulars by name and being able to experiment with new coffee blends and desserts without a corporate committee's approval.

"Honestly," I said, "I haven't had much time to think about it."

Hazel served up Jules's drink, her eyes darting between us with barely contained excitement.

Jules took a sip, her eyebrows rising in appreciation. "Mmm, this is delightful. Tell you what, I'd like to sweeten the deal a bit."

Hazel let out a tiny squeak beside me, which I pointedly ignored.

"Oh?" I said, my attention stirred despite myself.

Jules nodded, her voice lowering conspiratorially. "I want you to know, Parker, I'm not looking to be all 'corporate' about this. You'd have full autonomy to keep things authentic. Real. We'd simply be providing the resources to share your incredible products with a wider audience."

I felt a flutter of excitement in my stomach, quickly tempered by caution. "That sounds ... interesting. But why me? Why Catch You Latte?"

Jules smiled, gesturing around the cafe. "First, I may live in Charlotte, but this is my hometown. And I love that you are part of its revitalization. But from all the buzz and my research, it's clear you've captured lightning in a bottle here, Parker. Your coffee, this atmosphere—it's special. I think it could resonate far beyond Magnolia Grove."

I couldn't deny that I was intrigued. The idea of sharing my coffee with a wider audience without a bunch of suits looming over me was tempting. But could I do that without losing the small-town charm that made Catch You Latte special?

I continued nodding, buying myself time to think. "I appreciate the intriguing offer, Jules. It's certainly food for thought."

"Or drink for thought," Hazel cut in with a grin.

Jules chuckled. "Well, I won't pressure you for an answer now. Think it over. I'll be in town for another week." She produced a sleek business card from her portfolio and slid it across the counter. "Give me a call when you're ready to talk details."

As Jules made her way out the door, Hazel could barely contain herself. "Oh my gosh, Parker! This is huge!"

I picked up the card, turning it over in my hands. It was a tempting offer, no doubt. But as I looked around at the cozy cafe I'd built, at the familiar faces of my regulars, I wondered: was I ready to risk changing all this?

CHAPTER 5

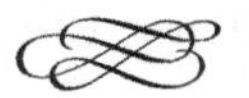

The best perk of living above Catch You Latte? The commute, hands down. No traffic jams, no icy roads to navigate—just a quick jaunt through the kitchen, up a flight of stairs, and voila! Home sweet home.

I stood by the window of my apartment, nursing a cup of my evening blend—a light decaf from Kenya's Nyeri region I labeled Sleepy-time Savior—and watched the streetlamps dot Main Street in a soft glow. Henderson's Hardware across the way was locking up for the night, and a few die-hard joggers were making their final laps around the square. In the distance, Magnolia Grove's water tower peeked above the tree line, a silent sentinel over our sleepy town.

The day had been a whirlwind of coffee orders and town gossip, punctuated by Hazel's non-stop chatter about Jules's offer. That girl could talk the ears off a cornfield if you let her. But now, as the town settled into its winter evening rhythm, it was finally Whit time.

Right on cue, a gentle knock echoed through my apartment. I opened the door to find Whit looking effortlessly handsome in a charcoal gray cardigan, holding up a bag that smelled like heaven itself.

"Daddy O's BBQ, as promised," he said with a grin.

I inhaled deeply, savoring the smoky aroma. "You, sir, are a true gentleman."

Who knew that pulled pork would become my new comfort food? Then again, in Magnolia Grove, surprises seemed to be the order of the day. As Whit set out our feast on the coffee table, I wondered what other surprises this evening might have in store.

Whit and I settled onto the couch, the tantalizing scent of barbecue filling the apartment. I took a bite of the pulled pork sandwich and let out an embarrassingly loud moan of appreciation.

Whit teased, "Daddy O's might just rival your coffee as Magnolia Grove's most addictive vice."

I pretended outrage, pointing my sandwich accusingly. "Them's fighting words, Hawthorne! Don't make me choose between coffee and BBQ—that's like asking a mother to favor one child!"

Whit chuckled, then his expression turned more serious. "About that text you sent me—Jules Winston floated a business offer your way?"

I sighed. "It is exciting. And terrifying. And confusing. I mean, expanding could be amazing, but ..."

"But you're worried about losing what makes Catch You Latte special," Whit finished for me.

I nodded, grateful as always for how well he understood me. "Exactly."

"The answer will come, Parker."

We sat in comfortable silence for a moment, enjoying our meals. The pulled pork barbecue melted in my mouth; its smoky sweetness was perfectly balanced by a tangy vinegar sauce that made my tastebuds dance. Golden-brown hush puppies, crispy on the outside and tender inside, practically begged to be dunked in the extra sauce pooling in my to-go container. The collard greens provided a pleasant bitter counterpoint, studded with bits of bacon that infused every bite with a rich, salty depth.

Then Whit spoke up. "You know, I've always wondered … how did someone as captivating as you never get swept off her feet and walked down the aisle?"

I smiled wryly. "City living, I suppose. Too busy chasing stories and crime scenes. Never slowed down enough to notice anyone special."

Whit dabbed his lips with a napkin. "I understand. I got caught up in college, then my PhD, and taking care of Mama before she passed. Time just slipped on by."

He glanced at me, his eyes softening. "I suppose I was just waiting for the right gal."

My pulse skittered. "I think I was waiting for the right guy," I replied, my voice barely above a whisper.

A moment of understanding hung between us, like a promise yet to be fulfilled.

My phone buzzed loudly, shattering the intimacy. I glanced at the screen and frowned. "Roger Buzzard? What could he want?"

"Only one way to find out," Whit said, gesturing for me to answer.

I took a deep breath and picked up the call. "Hello?"

"Ms. Hayes." Buzzard's nasally voice came through the speaker. "I hope I'm not interrupting your evening."

"Not at all," I lied, eyeing my cooling sandwich mournfully. "What can I do for you, Mr. Buzzard?"

The mental image hit me: Roger Buzzard perched behind his mahogany desk, fingers steepled like some cartoon villain. His beady eyes and thin-lipped smile had always reminded me more of a vulture than the legal eagle. Our last dealings during the Dylan Reeves case had left me with a lingering unease for his particular brand of lawyering.

Still, I couldn't deny the man's razor-sharp mind. He'd made a career of tap-dancing along the edge of the law without quite stepping over it. The running joke in town was that Roger Buzzard knew where all the bodies were buried in Magnolia Grove, and who owned the shovels. I hoped that was just a metaphor, though I wouldn't have been shocked if it wasn't.

"Ms. Hayes." Buzzard's voice pulled me back to the present. "I find myself in need of your ... unique skillset."

I raised an eyebrow, catching Whit's questioning look. "My barista skills? I wasn't aware you were a coffee enthusiast, Mr. Buzzard."

"Your investigative skills," he clarified. "It's about Lauren Yancey. I believe she's being framed, and I need your assistance to prove it."

"Don't they all say that, Roger?"

Buzzard's sigh crackled through the phone. "Ms. Hayes, I assure you, this is a frame job. Lauren has quite a disdain for firearms. She would sooner give up her favorite designer shoes than touch a gun. That gun was planted, I'm certain of it."

I caught Whit's eye, his eyebrows arched upward. "And why come to me? Surely, the great Roger Buzzard doesn't need help from a mere cafe owner."

"Because, Ms. Hayes, you have a knack for uncovering truths others overlook. And frankly, you're not bound by the same … limitations as law enforcement."

"You mean I'm willing to bend the rules?"

"I prefer to think of it as being creatively thorough," Buzzard replied smoothly. "Will you help? There is a sizable compensation should you accept."

"I'm not a licensed PI, Roger."

A pause hung on the line before Buzzard's voice resumed.

"Never mind those formalities. We will consider you a *consultant*." He drawled out the word *consultant*, giving it an air of importance.

"Consultant, right," I repeated dryly. "I'll think about it, Roger. Have a good night."

"Yes, you do that. Good evening."

I hung up and set my phone down.

Whit said, "Now pray tell, what was that all about?"

"Buzzard thinks Lauren is being framed. Wants me to consult, i.e., investigate. I'm not a PI, Whit. I'm just a coffee shop owner who occasionally does PI-type stuff."

Whit's lips quirked into a half-smile. "And you're

phenomenal at the PI-type stuff, Parker. You do have a gift for uncovering the truth."

I shook my head. "Maybe, but I can't take Buzzard's money. It feels ... wrong. Like I'd be covered in a layer of sleaze I'd never be able to wash off."

"I get that." Whit nodded. "But what if you didn't keep the money? I know some great local charities that could use the help."

I cocked my head, then reached over and mimed removing invisible glasses from his face. "Wait just a hot minute ... Could it be? The mysterious benefactor who donated half his inheritance to the children's home?" I gasped dramatically, pressing a hand to my chest. "All this time, mild-mannered town historian Whit Hawthorne was secretly Magnolia Grove's most generous philanthropist. The clues were there all along!"

Whit chuckled, a slight blush creeping up his neck. "I just believe in giving back, that's all. And hey, using Buzzard's money for good causes? That's a proper incentive, right?"

I leaned back, considering. The idea of using Buzzard's cash to help people in need did have a certain poetic justice to it. If Lauren was guilty, I'd still get paid. And if Lauren was innocent ...

"You're making this hard to resist, Whit. Using dubious compensation to fund saintly deeds? That's either utterly depraved or profoundly inspired. I think you might be a bad influence on me."

Whit touched my chin. "Just doing my part to keep

Magnolia Grove interesting. But ask yourself: are you ready to rejoin the amateur sleuthing fray?"

I hesitated, self-doubt creeping in. Was I ready? Born ready, perhaps. A brief, cynical thought flashed: Lauren's imprisonment might not be a bad thing. I swiftly pushed the thought aside. Sleuthing wasn't about personal feelings or biases; it was about uncovering the truth. If Lauren was guilty, I'd prove it. If innocent ... then justice demanded the real killer face the consequences.

I sighed dramatically, but I could feel the familiar excitement of a new case starting to bubble up. "I'm going to do it. But if this ends with me in a cheese vat, I'm blaming you."

"Deal." Whit laughed. "Now, let's finish this barbecue before it gets cold. Can't solve mysteries on an empty stomach, after all."

As we dug back into our sandwiches, I had to wonder what I was getting myself into. But with Whit by my side and the promise of helping others, maybe this would be an open-and-shut case.

Then again, this was Magnolia Grove. Things were never quite that simple.

THE NEXT MORNING, before the rush at my cafe, I left Hazel in charge and found myself at the door of Feta & Friends. The artisanal cheese shop sat a few doors up, its pristine storefront windows polished to a shine despite the winter frost creeping at the edges. Perfectly trimmed shrubs in copper planters flanked the entrance—Lauren's signature attention to detail was evident. A bitter wind whipped down Main Street, rattling the door and the "CLOSED" sign that hung on it. Behind the artfully arranged cheese displays, shadows moved in the dimly lit interior. I pulled my peacoat tighter, exhaled a visible puff of breath into the winter air, and knocked gently.

The door opened, and Sophia—Lauren's sprite of an assistant—peeked her head out. Her eager eyes lit up. "Good morning, Miss Hayes!"

"Morning, Sophia," I said, mustering my most charming smile. "I was hoping to catch Lauren. Is she in?"

Sophia hesitated for a moment, then seemed to make up her mind. She opened the door, ushering me in with a flourish that would have made Lauren proud. "We're just setting up for the day. Ms. Yancey is determined to keep the shop running, you know. Isn't she amazing?"

I bit back a snarky comment. "She's certainly … confident."

The buttery richness of brie softened the air while a faint whiff of smoky gouda lingered near the counter. Ethan barely looked up from a wheel of cheese he was fussing over, mumbling something about optimal aging conditions.

"Ms. Yancey is in the back office with Ms. Winston," Sophia informed me, her voice brimming with admiration. "They're discussing some very important business matters."

"I'll just wait here then," I said, moving toward the counter.

As Sophia busied herself with arranging a display of artisanal crackers, I casually made my way toward the back of the shop. The office door was slightly ajar, and voices drifted out. I inched closer, my coffee-slinger's instincts giving way to my inner detective.

"...I don't understand why you're being so difficult about this, Lauren." Jules's voice, usually so smooth, had an edge to it.

Lauren's reply was sharp. "Difficult? I'm being practical. Especially with a murder charge hanging over my head."

I leaned in closer.

"First, the Walter Carr deal fell through," Jules continued, frustration evident in her tone. "Now this. I might have to rethink our—"

"Rethink what?" Lauren interrupted. "Investing in the town pariah?"

There was a pause, and then Jules spoke again, her voice lowered. "Lauren, you didn't have anything to do with what happened to Walter, did you?"

My eyes widened. Was Jules pegging Lauren for murder?

"How dare you!" Lauren hissed. "I found the man exasperatingly rustic, annoyingly stubborn and always reeking of cow manure, but I had nothing to do with Walter's death."

Suddenly, the office door swung open fully. Lauren emerged first, her face a storm cloud of emotions, followed closely by Jules, who looked more composed but still tense.

Lauren's eyes glinted when she saw me. "Parker. Were you eavesdropping again?"

Before I could respond, Jules stepped forward, her demeanor shifting to polished charm.

"Parker! What a lovely surprise. I hope you've had time to consider our discussion."

Lauren's eyes flashed with unease. "Jules, are you ditching me for Parker?"

Jules's smile remained serene. "I have many horses in my stable, Lauren. Yours isn't my only interest."

I raised an eyebrow inwardly. Great, I was being compared to a horse.

"Actually," I began, "I'm here on a different matter—"

"She's probably here to gloat over my murder charge," Lauren cut in, her voice laced with sarcasm.

I took a deep breath. "Not exactly. I'm here because your lawyer, Roger Buzzard, asked me to look into your case."

Lauren's eyebrows shot up in surprise while Jules looked intrigued.

Jules inquired, "Roger asked you? Why?"

Lauren let out a derisive snort. "Oh, didn't you know? Parker here has a second job as the town snoop. She fancies herself a detective."

Jules's eyes lit up with interest. "Is that so? How fascinating."

We made our way into the main area of the cheese shop, Jules gathering her things off the counter as she prepared to leave.

"Parker, I hope you help clear up matters in this awful situation. And please don't forget to consider my offer,"

Jules said as she headed for the door. "I think we could do great things together. Lauren, we'll talk later."

As the bell jingled behind Jules, I turned back to Lauren, determined to get some answers. "Now, Lauren, about your case—"

"Sophia!" Lauren called out, interrupting me. "Make sure those camembert wheels are turned properly. And Ethan, bring out that new gouda batch. Here, Parker, try this." I watched in growing frustration as Lauren flitted between directing her employees and thrusting cheese samples at me.

"Mmm, yes, that's coming along nicely," Lauren murmured, sampling a piece of cheese. "Parker, what do you think of this one?"

"Lauren, this is serious. Can I please talk to you about your case?"

Lauren paused, a sample of cheese halfway to her mouth. For a moment, I saw a flicker of vulnerability in her eyes. Then it was gone, replaced by her usual haughty expression.

"Okay, so Buzzard hired you. I suppose that slick operator has his reasons. I'll play ball."

I gestured toward Sophia and Ethan. "Maybe we should do this in private?"

Lauren waved dismissively. "Sophia and Ethan? They're as loyal as they are … idealistic. I can trust them. Right, guys?"

Sophia's face lit up like a Broadway sign. "You bet, Ms. Yancey! I won't breathe a word!"

Ethan barely looked up from pressing cheese into molds. "Sure, yeah, whatever."

I pulled out my notepad and favorite rollerball gel pen from my bag, ready to dive in. "Alright, first question ... How do you suppose that Glock got into your handbag?"

Before answering me, Lauren turned to Sophia. "Make sure those brie wheels are at precisely 47 degrees Fahrenheit. Any warmer and they'll ripen too quickly."

"Right away, Ms. Yancey!" Sophia scurried off.

Lauren then addressed my question, her tone distracted. "I don't know how the gun got there. I know I didn't put it there. I wouldn't touch one of those vulgar instruments of death if you paid me. And if I did shoot Walter—which I didn't—do you think I'd be so stupid as to tote the thing around in my purse for anyone to find? I would've tossed it into the lake. Someone obviously planted it."

I darted a questioning glance at Sophia, then at Ethan, wondering if Lauren had considered them as potential suspects in planting the gun. Lauren intercepted my skeptical look and addressed my unspoken question.

"Them? No. Sophia has been with me for years and is loyal to a fault. She's probably never even seen a gun before the day of the festival. And Ethan? He's been too busy perfecting his artisanal cheeses to bother with sabotage. Besides, he's got a vested interest in the business; I've offered him a partnership."

I jotted this down in my notebook.

"Sophia!" Lauren yelled across the room. "When you're finished, please move the Swiss cheese to the window display. And answer this question: did you plant that gun in my purse?"

Sophia gave a curious tilt of her head, then responded in a calm and collected tone. "No."

"Ethan? What about you?" Lauren's tone was firm and controlled.

Ethan didn't look up from his work but shook his head, letting out a dismissive "pffft" as if irritated by the suggestion.

Lauren exhaled with a self-assured smile spreading across her face. "You see? My team is loyal and trustworthy."

I chose not to enlighten Lauren on the fundamentals of suspect interrogation, preferring to press on instead. "Do you have any idea who might want to frame you?"

Just then, something else caught Lauren's attention. "Ethan! That gouda needs to be rotated every six hours, not eight. Do try to keep up."

Ethan grumbled under his breath, "I am the expert, not you," then shuffled over to the cheese cave, his annoyance almost as potent as the odor of cheese.

Lauren's eyes lingered on Ethan, a flicker of irritation crossing her face before she turned back to me.

"What were you saying?"

"I asked if you knew anyone who might want to frame you…"

"Frame me? Half the town, probably. Success breeds jealousy, you know."

Lauren's inability to see her rude, off-putting behavior was mind-boggling. I moved on to my next question.

"What about this feud with Walter? There were tensions between you two for quite a while."

Lauren noticed something on one of the displays. "Sophia! The crackers should be arranged in a simple herringbone pattern, not that overly complicated design." Lauren huffed, then returned to our conversation. "The feud with Walter? Oh, it started in the fourth quarter of last year when I diversified my dairy sources. He'd assumed we were 'buddies' and took it personally when I made some fiscal decisions that affected him. But business is business, after all. That's much better, Sophia ..."

"Lauren," I said. "You're facing a murder rap. Can we please focus?"

Lauren picked up a cheese knife and raised it close as if looking at her reflection.

"Fine," she said, setting the knife back down. "What else do you want to know?"

I took a deep breath, ready to dig deeper. But as I formulated my next question, I wondered: was Lauren's distracted behavior a defense mechanism, or was she genuinely this unconcerned about being accused of murder?

"Where were you when Walter Carr was shot?" I poised my pen over my notepad.

Lauren rolled her eyes. "I can't say."

"Why not?"

"I don't know when he was shot."

"Fair point. Where were you between 1:30 and 2 PM?"

"I don't remember," Lauren replied confidently. "A lot was happening."

Sophia, who had been working on laying out the crackers in a herringbone pattern, piped up. "Wait, Ms. Yancey, remember that was when you—"

"Yes, Sophia." Lauren cut her off and shot her a look that could curdle milk. "Thanks for reminding me. I was offsite. I had to leave the festival to … run an errand." Then she thrust another piece of cheese at me. "Here, try this."

If I didn't know any better—and I did—I would've accused Lauren of deliberately trying to distract me. Still, I took the bite, and I had to admit it was good. The cheese melted on my tongue, its complex flavor dancing between nutty and slightly sweet with a subtle tang at the finish.

Lauren gave me a smug grin. "Pretty delish, huh? Anyway, to answer your question … I got back to my booth just after the whole fiasco with Walter. Right, Sophia?"

Sophia looked at Lauren, then me. "Um, yeah. That's right."

I swallowed, pushing aside my appreciation for the cheese. "What was the errand?"

Lauren's gaze sharpened. "I'd rather not say."

You can imagine my level of befuddlement. It seemed like she wanted me to think she was guilty.

I rubbed my forehead before continuing. "You're not making this easy, Lauren …"

"I thought you were some hot-shot investigative true-crime podcaster."

"Well, you're not exactly cooperating." I exhaled in frustration. "Okay, at least we can verify you were offsite by tracking your cell phone ... I'm sure Buzzard can get the records."

"Oh, I didn't have my phone. I left it at the booth," Lauren said in a clipped tone.

"Are you serious?!" I yelled. "I saw you on a call while I was investigating the crime scene."

"Yes, I'd returned, grabbed my phone from the booth and called the sign company to see about a refund. Then I saw the commotion down by the lake." Lauren's gaze drifted off, her voice taking on a distracted tone. "Hmm, pairing the truffle gouda with the fig and balsamic crackers ... no, too sweet. Maybe the aged cheddar with the rosemary and olive oil crackers instead?"

I slapped my notebook closed, frustration boiling over. How much more difficult was Lauren going to make this for me? Here we had the lead suspect, with a well-known feud with the victim, the weapon in her possession, and no verifiable alibi.

"Well, Lauren, clearly you're more interested in cheese than clearing your name. In my experience, you're looking at fifteen-to-life. You can let Buzzard know I'm done here."

Lauren's jaw dropped, her usual composure cracking for a moment. A flash of panic crossed her face before she regained control.

I turned on my heel and marched out of the shop, the bell above the door jingling behind me.

I had barely made it three steps when my phone buzzed. A text from an unknown number:

This goes deeper than you think. Stay out of it, coffee girl. This isn't amateur hour!

I rolled my eyes. "Really? A threatening and condescending text? How cliché."

This mystery person obviously didn't know me. Nothing sparked my defiance quite like someone trying to scare me away from something—especially while insulting my investigative skills. Sure, my stubbornness had landed me in some sticky situations before, but it was carved into my DNA like my coffee addiction and inability to keep my nose out of things.

Guilty or innocent, Lauren's case had just gotten a lot more interesting. Someone was challenging me to a game of chess, and this "coffee girl" intended to flip the board.

I spun around and marched right back into the cheese shop.

Lauren looked up with confusion etched on her face. "Forget something?"

I pocketed my phone, my determination crystallizing into resolve. "Yeah, I forgot that I'm constitutionally incapable of minding my own business. Looks like you're stuck with me, Lauren. We've got a case to crack."

CHAPTER 6

"What changed your mind?" Lauren asked.

I waved off her question, deciding not to mention the text I'd just received about dropping the case. "Let's just say I had a moment of clarity. Now, I'd like to talk to your employees. I'll start with Sophia. In private."

"You don't need to interview her in private; we're all like family," Lauren said.

I gave her a skeptical look. "Would you please let me do my job?"

Lauren's gaze lingered on me before she nodded. "Fine. Use my office." She gestured toward the hall that led to the back of her shop, her expression a mixture of reluctance and interest. "Sophia, go with Parker. She's got some questions to ask you."

"Will do, Lauren!"

Sophia led me down the hall, and we entered the office, the door clicking shut behind us. The space was a deliberate fusion of styles: modern lines and minimalist chic alongside whimsical cheese-inspired artwork. The sweet, heady aroma of designer perfume wafted through the air, subtly veiling the earthy scent of artisanal cheeses.

Sophia sat on a chair in front of Lauren's desk, hands folded neatly in her lap. "What would you like to know, Ms. Hayes?"

I took a seat in Lauren's chair at her desk, facing Sophia. I flipped open my notebook and held my pen. "Sophia, we've been acquainted with each other professionally since I got here last summer. But I don't really know you. Tell me a bit about yourself."

Sophia's face lit up, her enthusiasm spilling out. "I'm a Durham native. I studied business and psychology at Chapel Hill, then headed to New York. That's where I met Ms. Yancey, at an escape room I designed for a corporate event. I love escape rooms. Do you?"

"They're too easy."

"Oh, I agree! But the ones I crafted were different," Sophia said, a hint of pride and excitement creeping into her voice. "Most designers focus on the mechanical puzzles. I focus on the players themselves. Understanding their psychology and predicting their choices. My success rate was less than 2 percent."

"That's ... impressive?"

"People think escape rooms are about locks and codes." Her hands went from her lap to Lauren's desk, aligning a few pens into perfect parallel lines. "But they're really about human behavior. Every room tells a story. The trick is making people think they're writing it themselves, when really ..." She caught herself, that familiar meek demeanor sliding back into place. "Sorry. I get carried away talking about my old work."

"No, please continue. It's fascinating."

"Well …" She glanced at the door, then lowered her voice. "Take you, for instance. You're methodical but intuitive. You notice details others miss—like just now when you tracked my hand arranging these pens." A small smile formed at her lips. "You'd approach a puzzle room differently than, say, Lauren, who'd demand hints and get frustrated when things aren't straightforward. Or Jesse, who'd try to force solutions …"

"You've given this a lot of thought." I tucked my hair behind my ear.

"Observation is a habit." She shrugged, then added almost absently, "Like how you tuck your hair behind your ear when you're piecing something together. Or how you get that little crinkle between your eyebrows when something doesn't add up." Her eyes met mine, sharp and analytical, before quickly dropping back to her demure pose. "Sorry. Professional hazard from my psychology student days. Anyway, Lauren saw those strengths in me and took me under her wing. We worked together on Wall Street until she decided to open Feta & Friends down here. I couldn't pass up the chance to come back to my home state and be part of her vision."

"You like working for her?"

Her eyes danced with delight. "Yes! Ms. Yancey has taught me many things. She is my mentor and my inspiration. I've learned *sooo* much from her."

I suppressed a sarcastic reply, something about learning

the art of the hostile takeover and other ruthless business tactics. Old habits die hard, but I was working on it. So, I just nodded, jotting some notes.

"That's terrific. Now, can you walk me through the time at the festival leading up to finding Walter's body? Lauren mentioned she went on an errand?"

Sophia's fingers arranged a pad of sticky notes on Lauren's desk. "Yes, she left a bit before 1:30 PM and got back around 1:55 PM."

"Why did she go? Why not you?"

Sophia shrugged. "I don't know. She said she needed to take care of something private."

"And she didn't take her phone?"

"No. She left her purse at the booth."

"What else do you remember around that time? Anything that could help?"

Sophia's brows crinkled in thought. "I remember seeing Jesse Carr stumbling by, muttering something about cheese. It looked like he was heading toward the lake—sort of in the direction where … well, you know, where they found Walter's body."

My pen hovered over the notebook. "What time was this?"

"Not sure. It was after Lauren had left, though … A little later, I saw him stumbling around behind the booth. He tripped over our extension cord, causing our space heater to go out. Super annoying because it was so cold that day."

I remembered seeing Jesse Carr standing behind the booths when I was tossing some trash.

I leaned in closer. "Could Jesse have planted the gun in Lauren's bag?"

Uncertainty flashed in Sophia's widened eyes. "Maybe? I don't know."

"Where was Ethan during this?" I asked.

Sophia shrugged. "He left way before that. Went down to talk to people and watch the Polar Plunge."

"You didn't want to join him?"

She shook her head with a hint of distaste. "No thanks. Watching people jump into freezing water isn't my thing."

I shifted gears. "What about the graffiti on the sign? Any idea how that happened?"

"No clue. It was here in the shop when I arrived that morning. I assumed the sign company delivered it. The container tube had been lying out the entire morning while we were setting up, but I didn't look at it until we took it out at the festival. That's my fault. I should've inspected it. I really let Lauren down." Sophia's face fell with regret.

"Don't be too hard on yourself. Think someone at the sign company might've done it? Or Walter himself?"

Sophia's shoulders rose in a shrug. "Could've been anyone, really. Lauren's business practices rub certain people the wrong way. The delivery driver, maybe?"

"What about Ethan?"

"What about him?"

"Think he's capable of any of this?"

Sophia's face grew intense. "I don't think he'd do anything like that! Lauren just offered him part of the business."

"Lauren mentioned that."

"Yes. He's been working super hard, and he's very good at what he does. I'm happy for him." She paused, her gaze flickering briefly to the side. "He might seem a bit ... self-assured, but he'd never do anything to jeopardize Lauren or the business. Especially frame her for murder."

I nodded thoughtfully. "One more question. I overheard Jules and Lauren discussing a failed deal to buy Walter's farm. Do you know anything about that?"

Sophia beamed with psychology-major pride. "Jules Winston is fascinating from a behavioral standpoint. Brilliant business mind, but there's this ... underlying need to prove herself. You see it in her rapid expansion patterns, her aggressive acquisition strategies." Sophia's voice took on an analytical tone. "Classic overcompensation for childhood instability. She builds empires because she couldn't control her environment growing up. That drive makes her ... predictable."

She caught herself, that familiar meek demeanor sliding back into place. "But that's just my armchair analysis. Like I said, I can get carried away in that stuff. I probably shouldn't psychoanalyze the boss's business partner."

I tapped my pen against the notebook, thinking. "So, you don't know anything about the farm deal going south?"

"Oh, well. No."

"Alright, Sophia. Thanks for your time. I might have more questions later. Could you ask Ethan to come in here?"

"Certainly." She got up and left.

A moment later, Ethan shuffled in, his gaze fixed on some distant point over my shoulder. "Sophia said you wanted to talk?" His tone was flat.

I gestured to the chair Sophia had vacated. "Thanks for coming in, Ethan. I just have a few questions."

He slumped into the seat, crossing his arms. "What do you want to know?"

"Let's start with your background. How did you end up working for Lauren?"

Ethan's posture straightened slightly, a hint of pride creeping into his voice. "I moved from France when I was five to Cedarburg, Wisconsin. Learned everything about cheese there. Then I went to New York and worked for Jean-Claude Fromage."

He paused, eyeing me with a mixture of expectation and disdain. When I didn't react, he added, "The world-renowned cheese guru? But I suppose you wouldn't know about that."

I bit back a retort. "Right. And Lauren?"

"Met her through industry events. She wanted to break into cheese but barely knew camembert from brie." He snorted. "However, she has a shrewd business mind, I'll give her that. I joined her over a year and a half ago, and voilà! Here we are."

"Rumor has it she offered you a stake in the company?"

Ethan nodded, beaming with more pride. "Ten percent."

I scribbled some notes. "Are you accepting?"

"Of course. I'm no idiot."

"No, you're not. What do you remember from around the time Walter was murdered?"

Ethan's eyes glazed over slightly. "Not much. I was busy with the cheeses, explaining the complex flavor profiles to customers who probably couldn't tell the difference between artisanal and processed."

"Do you remember seeing Jesse Carr?"

"You mean his outburst on the stage?"

"After that."

"Vaguely remember seeing him stumbling around ..."

"What about when he tripped over the extension cord?"

"First I'm hearing of that. I must've left the booth before that happened."

"Where did you go?"

"To wish Maggie good luck before she did the Polar Plunge." A flicker of emotion crossed his face before it settled back into indifference.

"Maggie Thomas? Why?"

Ethan squinted and folded his arms across his narrow chest. "I like her, okay? She's nice. And I think she might feel the same way."

I decided not to respond with sarcasm. Ever since Maggie's recent spiritual awakening, she'd been radiating a new level of warmth and kindness. But was she genuinely interested in Ethan, or was he simply misreading her newfound enthusiasm for spreading joy?

"Okay ... Now, do you remember when Lauren left to run that errand?"

Ethan's forehead wrinkled. "I wasn't paying attention. I was busy with the cheese samples, then I went to the dock to watch the Polar Plunge."

"What about the sign? Who do you think is the culprit?"

He shrugged. "No clue."

"And the ongoing static with Walter Carr? Any thoughts on that?"

"Not my department. I'm just the cheese guy, remember? Lauren and Walter had their differences, but I stayed out of it. She's all about the bottom line; he was old-school, always talking about handshakes and friendships."

"What about Sophia? What's your take on her?" I asked.

Ethan's smile was laced with condescension. "She worships Lauren, wants to follow in her footsteps with the business. Smart, but a bit … an eager beaver."

"Did Lauren offer her a partnership?"

Ethan shook his head. "Not that I know of, but I wouldn't be surprised if it happens soon. Sophia's got potential."

I processed his words.

"One last thing. Have you heard anything about expansion plans for the business?"

For the first time, Ethan showed a flicker of interest. "Lauren and Jules have been talking about some bigger vision. Multiple locations, maybe. Whatever they want to do, I'm on board."

"Thanks, Ethan. That's it for now."

I TOLD Lauren I'd talk to her later, and I stepped out of Feta & Friends, the crisp winter air biting at my cheeks. My mind whirled with questions.

Lauren's nonchalance bothered me. Earlier, I'd been

convinced of her innocence, but Sophia's interview had me doubting again. Could Sophia be covering for Lauren? Ethan didn't strike me as someone who'd frame his boss, but he also could've been covering for her. After all, didn't Lauren say they were like family? One slightly dysfunctional and complicated family …

Time for the next move.

I pulled out my phone and texted Whit.

Busy?

Listening to Delacroix's tunnel stories … for the 3rd time lol.

Whit's humor was infectious.

Need a break?

You know it. What's up?

I need a ride to visit Jesse Carr. Pick me up?

I'll be out front of CYL in 5 minutes …

I made my way down to the cafe and popped in, where Hazel bustled around, preparing for the morning rush. Her mint-colored hair bobbed as she meticulously arranged cheesecakes and some muffins in the display case, singing a tune.

"Think you can handle the morning rush by yourself, Hazel?"

She froze, her cheesecake arrangement stalled. "Uhhh, sure?" Her voice climbed an octave higher than usual.

"I promise to give you a nice bonus."

"Really? I mean, yes! Absolutely! I've got this!" The cheesecake made it safely to its destination.

Guilt niggled at my conscience as I watched her square her shoulders with determination. Hazel had reduced her studies at Magnolia Valley to part time so she could work more hours at the cafe. The decision had sparked a three-day debate between us, with me insisting education came first and her arguing that real-world experience upstaged textbooks any day.

The girl had more dedication in her pinky finger than most people had in their whole body. Though sometimes, her enthusiasm for baking resulted in what looked like a flour bomb explosion in the kitchen. The cleaning service —me—had threatened to quit on many occasions.

A car horn interrupted my musings. Through the window, I spotted Whit's sedan idling at the curb.

"Remember," I called out to Hazel, "the morning rush lives and dies by the espresso machine. And please try not to turn the kitchen into a complete war zone."

"Got it, boss!" She gave me a mock salute, then immediately knocked over a stack of coffee cup sleeves.

I exited the cafe and slid into the passenger seat of Whit's car, grateful for the warmth.

"So, what's the latest?" Whit asked as he pulled away from the curb.

I filled him in on the mysterious text and my conversations with an aloof Lauren, eager Sophia and indifferent Ethan, their vagueness and unwillingness to provide Lauren's alibi.

"Something feels off. And now we've got expansion plans and a failed farm deal ... then add a loose cannon like Jesse Carr into the mix."

Whit's expression grew somber. "Jesse wasn't in his right mind that day, that's for sure. Growing up, we were thick as thieves running in the same pack. After his mom,

Becky, left, he started down a rough path. Lost his way, you know? Became a wild card."

"Why'd his mom leave?"

"Felt dairy farming wasn't her calling. Her heart was in acting, so she moseyed off to Hollywood to pursue stardom." Whit's voice softened. "When Jesse's not drinking, he's got a good heart. Problem is ... those moments are few and far between. I've tried to stay in touch, be a steady friend, but it's gotten tougher. That's why Walter refused to pass on the farm to him. But I don't know if Jesse would kill his father over it."

I looked out the window at the passing storefronts that dotted the charming town of Magnolia Grove. "You throw years of bitterness, resentment and alcohol into the mix ... anything can happen."

We drove to the outskirts of town, where Magnolia Grove's quaint charm shifted to humbler residences. Wheeler's Haven Mobile Home Park unfolded before us, its well-manicured lawns and neat homes a testament to pride of ownership. But Jesse's trailer told a different story. Pulling up, we saw peeling paint and a yard cluttered with discarded odds and ends, a defiant contrast to the park's otherwise tidy atmosphere. But amidst the disarray, one thing stood out: a brand-new gleaming silver Chevy Silverado, its chrome wheels and sparkling windows a beacon of opulence in a sea of neglect.

"Looks like Jesse's doing alright for himself," Whit said, raising an eyebrow as he killed the engine.

I shook my head. "No way he got that from any life insurance payout if there was one. Not that fast."

"Unless he took out a loan, anticipating the payout," Whit suggested, skeptical.

"But that would mean he planned ahead," I said, my mind buzzing with implications. "And that raises a whole lot of questions."

Whit's expression turned serious. "You ready to ask those questions?"

I took a deep breath. "As ready as I'll ever be to interview a grieving, possibly drunk son who may or may not have planted a gun on the current prime suspect."

We stepped out of the car. Gravel crunched underfoot as we approached Jesse's trailer. Whit's hushed voice preceded our ascent up the creaky steps to the weathered porch. "Let me start. I know how to connect with him, or at least, I did."

I nodded, grateful for Whit's insight. He'd grown up with Jesse, but even more so, he had a gentle way of connecting with people that I sometimes lacked. I was working on it, though.

Whit lightly rapped his knuckles against the screen door. We waited, listening for any signs of life inside. After a moment, we heard shuffling footsteps and muffled cursing.

As the door swung open, Jesse Carr stood before us, looking like he'd just rolled out of bed. His hair was unkempt, his eyes red-rimmed, and his bare chest sported a map of scars and tattoos. Faded jeans clung to his hips, but his overall appearance screamed rough night, or better yet, rough fifteen years.

"Whit?" Jesse's voice was gravelly as he rubbed his eyes. "What're you doin' here, man?"

"Hey, Jesse," Whit said, his voice gentle. "Mind if we come in? We'd like to talk to you about your dad."

Jesse's face clouded over. "What's there to talk about? He's dead, ain't he?"

I scooted closer to the door and chimed in, "We're trying to figure out what happened. We thought you might be able to help."

Jesse's gaze shifted to me, suspicion crawling. "Who's she?"

"This is Parker Hayes," Whit explained. "She's helping with the investigation."

Jesse snorted. "Right. The coffee lady turned detective. Heard about you." He stepped back, waving us in with a sarcastic flourish. "Well, come on in, then. Welcome to my humble abode."

The screen door creaked open, then slapped shut behind us, enveloping us in the dimly lit lair. The trailer's interior was a mix of clutter and attempted order. A laundry basket overflowed, yet the kitchen counters gleamed. Jesse closed the front door and gestured to the living room. There, a sprawling couch, recliner and coffee table, topped with a bowl of chips, faced a massive 70-inch TV dominating the wall.

Jesse rummaged through the laundry basket, pulling out his cleanest dirty shirt. He examined it briefly, sniffed the collar and, seemingly satisfied, buttoned it on.

"Y'all want something to eat? Got chips," Jesse offered, pointing to the coffee table. "And beef jerky."

"Sure, I'll take some jerky, thanks," I replied impulsively.

Whit politely declined.

Jesse walked into the adjacent kitchen, grabbed a package and tossed me a bag labeled "Crazy Carl's Jerky Co.—Tear It Up, Y'all!" The name raised an eyebrow, but I opened it anyway.

"My buddy Carl makes that," Jesse said proudly. "Best jerky in three counties."

The first bite of Crazy Carl's Jerky was a flavor bomb—rich, smoky and savory. But the texture? That was a different story. It was as if I'd taken a bite out of a vintage cowboy boot, worn and weathered to perfection. I chewed, my jaw muscles protesting the exertion.

"Good, huh?" Jesse asked.

I gave him a thumbs-up, my mouth still locked in a battle with the stubborn jerky.

Jesse gestured to the couch and then slumped back into the recliner, munching on potato chips. Whit and I perched awkwardly on the edge of the sagging couch.

"So," Jesse said, his voice rough, "what do you want to know?"

Whit leaned forward, his elbows on his knees. "Jesse, we're sorry about your dad. We know this must be tough for you."

Jesse's face hardened. "Yeah, well, life's tough all over, ain't it?" He chomped on a potato chip.

I nodded, still working on the same piece of jerky. At this rate, I'd be chewing all day. I focused on taking in the details of Jesse's living space. The walls revealed his personality and history. A faded map of North Carolina hung alongside a worn NASCAR poster, while shelves displayed mementos. A dusty frame held a cherished photo: young Jesse and his dad, Walter Carr, standing proudly beside a prize-winning cow, beaming with joy. Scattered touches—lace curtains, floral cushions—hinted at a woman's influence.

Whit continued, his voice gentle but firm. "We need to know what you remember from the day of the festival. Anything you can tell us might help."

Jesse ran a hand through his greasy hair. "I told the deputies everything already. I was three sheets to the wind, okay? Can't remember squat."

"You were seen near Lauren Yancey's booth," I interjected. "You tripped over their extension cord."

His bloodshot eyes narrowed. "So what if I did? That don't mean nothin'."

Whit shot me a look that clearly said, "Let me handle this." He turned back to Jesse. "We're not accusing you of anything, Jesse. We're just trying to piece everything together. Your dad and Lauren had some issues, right? Can you tell us about that?"

Jesse let out a bitter laugh. "Issues? That's one way to put it. That city slicker was lowballing my dad. And now she's got his blood on her hands."

I leaned forward, my interest piqued. "What makes you say that, Jesse?"

"Driving him out of business. Forcing him to sell the farm." Suddenly, his face contorted with anger. "You know what? Screw it. I'm sick of you city slickers comin' in here, thinkin' you own everything!"

Whit held up a hand, trying to calm Jesse down. "We're just trying to help—"

"Help?" Jesse snorted. "Like that city slicker was 'helping' when she threw money my way to walk this way and that way? Now my pops is dead!"

I paused mid-chew, my attention snapping to Jesse. What was he talking about? Was he just in a state of delirium now? The jerky forgotten, I managed to swallow the leathery mass. "What do you mean? Someone offered you money? Lauren?"

Jesse's face reddened, his voice dripping with venom. "You city folks think you're so big, tossin' bucks around like it's confetti. Well, let me tell you, Jesse Carr ain't no pushover."

I cut through his tirade. "Who was throwing money at you?"

He whooshed his hand and grumbled. "I'm just speakin' figuratively. Y'all act the same."

Whatever he was getting at made little to no sense. I cut straight to the chase. "Did your dad have a life insurance policy?"

Jesse's eyes flashed, and he slammed his fist on the coffee table, making the bowl of potato chips jump and scatter. Crunchy shards flew everywhere, some landing in his lap, others on the floor. His face twisted in rage, the veins on his neck bulging. He leaned forward, his elbows on the table, his hands clenched into fists.

"You think I killed my papa for the money?" Jesse's voice trembled, barely controlled. "That Cheez Whiz peddler did it, and I aim to pin it—no matter what it takes."

His words echoed in my mind … "Pin it? Pin it on Lauren?"

"I didn't say 'pin it,' I said, 'prove it.' Like, prove she did it. 'Cause she did."

I decided not to argue his word choice. The situation was already volatile. No need to poke an already angry bear.

Suddenly, a crash echoed from the back of the trailer. Jesse's bloodshot eyes widened, and he stumbled to his feet.

"What was that?" I asked.

Just as Jesse was about to respond, an attractive woman who looked to be in her thirties emerged from the back room, wearing a faded T-shirt that read, *I'm not arguing, I'm just explaining why I'm right*. She was in the act of pulling up her wavy amber hair into a messy top knot.

"Hey, babe, why you raisin' Cain out here?" she asked, her pale green eyes sparkling with amusement. Then, noticing Whit and me, her animated expression turned curious. "Oh, I didn't know we had company."

Jesse cleared his throat and grumbled, "They're just leavin'."

But she was already moving toward us, her petite hand extended. "Hi, I'm Amber. You have really pretty hair!" She beamed at me. "You should come by my salon and let me do you up. What's your name?"

"I'm Parker," I replied, charmed by her warmth. "I'll have to take you up on that offer, Amber."

Jesse's impatience grew. "Time for y'all to go."

Whit's eyes locked onto Jesse's, and with deep sincerity, he said, "Jesse, come on. We've known each other a long time. We're trying to help figure out who killed your dad."

"Yeah, well, with friends like you, who needs death and taxes?" Jesse said. "Amber's gotta get to work, and I got matters to attend to."

As we stood to leave, Amber's green eyes twinkled as she fiddled with her messy top knot. "Oh, if y'all wanna help, y'all should talk to Ronald Sweetwater, the owner of that cute little ice cream shop downtown, Sweet Scoops. He was knee-deep in strong-arming Jesse's daddy, bless his heart."

Jesse's expression turned tense, his voice low and warning. "Amber, honey, don't."

But Amber continued, her voice bubbly and full of Southern charm. "Aww, come on, Jesse. I'm just tellin' it like it is. Ronald's got a smile as sweet as candy corn, but he's got a mind slicker than a snake's belly. My daddy said you can't trust him as far as you can throw him. And let me tell you, he's got a history with my family. Why, he even took a shot at my daddy once!"

Jesse's face reddened, his eyes glinting with anger. "Amber, that's enough."

Amber's grin faltered, but she quickly recovered, her smile brightening again. "Oh, okay. I better get ready for work. Busy day ahead!"

Jesse brushed chip shards from his shirt and approached the door. He swung it open, then pushed the screen door wide, his expression expectant.

Whit nodded sympathetically at Amber. "Miss Amber, nice meeting you." He turned to Jesse. "Take care, Jesse."

I followed suit, extending the bag of jerky toward Jesse. "Nice meeting you all. Appreciate the enlightening conversation."

Jesse nodded curtly and pointed to the bag of jerky in my hand. "Keep it."

As we stepped out onto the small porch, Amber called out, waving brightly. "Bye! Nice meetin' y'all! Come on by the salon sometime, Parker! Amber's Hair Affairs on Vance."

The screen door slapped shut behind us, the sound sharp and final, leaving us standing on the creaking wooden porch.

We overheard Jesse's hushed reprimand, muffled but still audible. "Why'd you gotta run your mouth off, Amber? You know better than to stir up trouble."

Amber's response was defiant yet somehow sweet. "Well, they need to know the truth!"

Their argument faded into the distance as we walked back to the car.

This case was getting more tangled by the minute, and I had a feeling Crazy Carl's Jerky wasn't the only tough thing I'd be chewing on for a while.

CHAPTER 7

I leaned back in the passenger seat of Whit's sedan, my mind churning over our conversation with Jesse. The car's heater fought valiantly against the winter chill seeping through the windows.

"What do you think?" Whit asked, his eyes fixed on the road ahead.

I sighed. "Jesse's a mess, but I don't think he killed his father. He seemed genuinely upset, beneath all that bravado."

Whit nodded. "Agreed. And that rambling bit about someone paying him?"

"I couldn't tell if he was being literal or not. Might be something to look into." I tapped my fingers on the armrest. "So, what's next? Want to go have a chat with Ronald Sweetwater at Sweet Scoops?"

"Sounds like a plan."

I straightened up, a thought striking me. "Actually, let's make a pit stop first. Walter's farm."

Whit quirked an eyebrow. "Why? We don't have a warrant or anything."

"My gut says we need to check it out," I replied, my tone leaving no room for argument.

Whit shrugged and made a left turn, heading toward the outskirts of town. Soon, we were pulling into the gravel driveway of Walter's farmhouse. The place looked eerily quiet, no longer the bustling dairy operation it had no doubt been just last week.

We pulled up to Walter's farm, the gravel crunching under Whit's tires. A familiar black-and-white cow stood near the fence, eyeing us with what I swore was recognition.

"Is that the infamous Bessie?" I asked, nodding toward the bovine.

Whit chuckled. "The one and only. Looks like she's behaving herself today."

"Let's hope she doesn't decide to take another stroll down the road," I muttered as we got out of the car. I strode toward the front door, Whit trailing behind me.

"Parker, what are you doing?" he asked.

I tried the doorknob. "It's unlocked," I announced, pushing the door open.

Whit hesitated for a moment before following me inside. The house smelled of old wood and something I couldn't quite place—maybe loneliness, if that had a scent.

We crept through the living room, our footsteps echoing on the ancient wood flooring. Suddenly, a noise from deeper in the house made us freeze.

"Someone's here," Whit whispered, his eyes wide.

I pressed a finger to my lips and motioned for him to follow me. We inched toward the kitchen, my heart pounding so loud I was sure whoever was in the house could hear it.

As we reached the kitchen doorway, I took a deep breath and peered around the corner. The sight that greeted me made me wonder if I was dreaming.

An old man in overalls and a tweed newsboy cap stood at the counter with his back to us, humming tunelessly as he slathered strawberry jam on a slice of bread. He turned suddenly, and I let out an embarrassingly high-pitched yelp.

The old man, startled by my outburst, spun around, knocking over an empty coffee mug. It clattered across the counter but didn't break.

"Sweet mother of pearl!" he exclaimed, clutching his chest. "You nearly scared me half to death!"

I stepped forward, hands raised in a placating gesture. "We're so sorry, sir. We didn't mean to startle you."

The old man squinted at us. His face was a roadmap of life's adventures, deep laugh lines framing his warm brown eyes. His face lit up in recognition. "Whit Hawthorne?!"

Whit grinned, stepping forward to shake his hand. "Good to see you, Mr. Pickler. It's been a while. How's that sinkhole in your back forty?"

"Still trying to swallow my tractor every chance it gets," Pickler chuckled. He looked at me. "Let me guess. You must be the infamous Parker Hayes. Clyde Honeycutt has told me all about you!"

I smiled, remembering that my handyman had brought up "his ol' buddy Pickler" on more than one occasion. Clyde was always helping Pickler with some property issue or another. "Clyde's mentioned you as well."

"Well, what in tarnation are you doing here?" Pickler righted the fallen mug and pulled out a handkerchief to wipe up the few drops of coffee that had spilled.

"Mr. Pickler, we're trying to figure out what happened to Walter. Why are you at Walter's house?"

He took off his cap and rubbed his curly salt-and-pepper hair. "Such a shame about Walter. Was fixin' to retire and go on some cruises. Even promised to bring me along on one, courtesy of the sale of this property." Pickler's expression turned wistful. "Now, to answer your question, young lady, I'm here just caretaking until all this estate malarkey gets sorted."

"Ah. Got it. Do you know if Walter was okay with selling? Or was he bitter?" I asked.

"Bitter? Heavens, no!" Pickler replied, absently straightening a stack of farm magazines on the counter. "Walter was thrilled. For years he'd talked about the changing business landscape. He wanted out while the market was hot."

My ears perked up. Walter's enthusiasm for selling contradicted Jesse's account. "You wouldn't happen to know who was interested in buying the farm, would you?"

Pickler scratched his chin, his weathered hands bearing the calluses of decades of farm work. "Sure. Once word got out he was thinking of selling, Walter had plenty of offers. That fancy lady from Charlotte was sniffing around, and of course, there was Ronald Sweetwater. You just missed him."

Whit and I exchanged glances. "Ronald was here?" Whit asked.

"Sure was," Pickler confirmed, ambling over to the wall to fiddle with the antiquated thermostat. "Trying to find the agreement he claims he and Walter signed."

I felt a surge of excitement. This was exactly the kind of lead we'd been hoping for. "Did he find it?"

Pickler shook his head, giving up on the thermostat. "Nope. Looked high and low but came up empty-handed." He grabbed his coffee mug and frowned at its emptiness. "Where's my manners? Y'all want some coffee?" He filled the mug with tap water, dumped in a spoonful of instant grounds and popped it in the microwave.

"No thanks," I said, fighting to keep my professional coffee-making sensibilities in check.

Whit cleared his throat. "I'm good, thank you."

"Do you know where Walter might've kept important documents like that?" I steered us back on track.

A twinkle of amusement flickered in his eyes. "Well, now, that's the million-dollar question, ain't it? Walter always was a bit ... particular about his paperwork."

Whit chimed in. "Particular how?"

Pickler glanced around as if checking for eavesdroppers, then lowered his voice. "Walter had himself a special place for keeping important stuff. Someplace he reckoned was safe from fire, flood and ..." He paused for dramatic effect. "Soviet invasion."

I blinked, wondering if I'd heard him right. "I'm sorry, did you say Soviet invasion?"

The microwave dinged. Pickler retrieved his mug, took a long sip and nodded. "Sure did. And believe you me, Walter wasn't taking any chances."

I STOOD at the edge of Walter's dairy farm, winter's chill casting a barren landscape, the only sound a lone *mooooo* drifting through the crisp air. We stood in front of a rusted metal door of what looked like the entrance of a storm shelter nestled within a large grassy mound.

"Well, there she is," Pickler announced, gesturing to the door with a flourish. "Walter's pride and joy. The Fort Knox of Magnolia Grove."

Whit let out a low whistle. "Not very cheerful looking."

I approached the door, my shoes crunching in the cold grass. "So, this is where Walter kept all his important documents?"

Pickler touched the brim of his cap and nodded. "Yup. Said it was the only place safe from—"

"Fire, flood and Soviet invasion," I finished for him. "You mentioned that."

The old caretaker fumbled with a set of keys and, after a moment of jangling, found the right one and inserted it into the lock.

"Now, I gotta warn you," Pickler said, turning to face us with a wide grin. "Could be a bit ... surprising."

I braced myself, expecting the worst. Pickler turned the

key, and with a groan that sounded like the ghosts of a thousand rusted hinges, the door swung open.

A wave of warm air hit us, carrying the scent of cedar, leather and pipe tobacco.

Pickler reached inside and flicked a switch. Soft lighting illuminated a space that looked more like a cozy den than a Cold War bunker.

"Good gravy," I muttered, taking in the scene.

The walls were lined with polished wooden shelves, neatly organized with canned goods and beverages. On another shelf were labeled binders and file boxes. A small kitchenette occupied one corner, complete with a vintage percolator and mini fridge. In the center, a worn leather armchair sat beside a side table stacked with books and magazines.

Whit stepped inside and marveled at the place. "This is not what I expected."

I followed him in, my gaze sweeping the surprisingly inviting space. "Okay, I'm officially confused. This looks more like a man cave than a bomb shelter."

Pickler chuckled from the doorway. "Clyde and I helped him gussy it up a few years back. Walter said if he was gonna spend time in here organizing his papers or ridin' out a storm, might as well be comfortable."

I brushed my fingers against the labeled binders.

The old man's weathered face cracked into a grin. "Walter was particular. Everything's filed by year and topic."

"Well, that makes our job easier." Whit was already scanning the shelves with intrigue.

Like Whit, I was excited to dig into this unexpectedly pleasant archive. "Why didn't you tell Ronald about this?"

Pickler's face grew serious. "A few days before Walter was murdered, he confided in me that he was having second thoughts about selling to Ronald. Said he wanted to look into something, I'm not sure what though. So, I reckoned I'd better leave it be."

Whit looked up from a stack of folders he was examining. "Then why tell us?"

Pickler's eyes crinkled with his trademark warmth. "Whit, I tossed horseshoes with your daddy for years, and I've known you since you were knee-high to a squirrel. I know your character. If anyone can sort this mess out, it's you and our little gumshoe here, Parker."

I decided to let the "little gumshoe" comment slide and focused on the task at hand. Whit and I methodically worked our way through the shelves, checking dates and labels.

Pickler excused himself, asking again if we wanted any coffee. We politely declined.

We dug into the files, scanning dates and labels and documents. I pulled some paperwork out of a folder and read through it.

"Well, well, well … Looks like Jesse's not going to get any life insurance payout anytime soon."

Whit took the document and read through it. "The policy … Hmm, certain non-negotiable stipulations apply … maintaining good behavior, staying out of legal trouble and regular attendance at Alcoholics Anonymous meetings …"

"Yeah … I'm guessing he's not going to meet those terms."

"You never know, Parker." Whit went back to digging through the folders. A moment later, Whit spoke up. "Found something."

I looked over.

Whit held out a sheet of paper titled "Promise to Sell—Carr Dairy Farm."

I scanned the page. "This is it. The agreement with Ronald Sweetwater. Dated the week before Walter's murder."

Whit pointed to a yellow sticky note. "Looks like Walter signed it, but look at the note."

On the sticky note, in what I assumed was Walter's scrawl, was written: "Before Ronnie signs, check into his alleged 'development' plans. NO HOUSING DEVELOPMENTS!"

"Housing developments?" I wondered aloud.

"Lots of farms around have been selling out to developers. Maybe ol' Ronnie had plans to do just that," Whit suggested.

"And that would've made Walter pause on the sale …"

"Certainly would have." Whit carefully placed the document back in its folder. He handed the folder to me. "Looks like our visit with Ronald is about to get a lot more interesting."

"Yep. And I'm craving a scoop of cold, hard truth—extra sprinkles, please."

"You think Ronald's aiming to scoop out more than just profits?"

I playfully punched his shoulder. "You're starting to sound like my dad—let's leave the corny quips in his territory."

~

SWEET SCOOPS WAS JUST a stone's throw from my cafe. Although I'd indulged in their treats occasionally since moving to Magnolia Grove, this was my first visit since fall. I knew Ronald Sweetwater, the owner, casually.

As I pushed open the door, a cheerful electronic bell announced our arrival. Warm air enveloped us, a welcoming escape from January's biting chill.

Ronald stood behind the counter organizing stacks of sugar cones. His round, cherubic face and neatly combed silver hair exuded a simple put-together appearance. His ever-present smile and crisp white apron—adorned with the shop's logo, a grinning ice cream cone wearing sunglasses—made him seem plucked from a Norman Rockwell painting.

"Well, if it isn't Parker Hayes and Whit Hawthorne!" Ronald's voice was as smooth as his soft serve. "What brings you two in on this frosty day?"

"Just thought we'd stop by for a scoop," I said, eyeing the flavors in the display case. "What's good today?"

Ronald's eyes lit up. "Oh, you've got to try our new Magnolia White Chocolate Chip Cookie Dough. It's killer."

I winced internally at his poor choice of words but nodded. "Sounds great. I'll take a scoop."

Whit raised an eyebrow at me. "Ice cream? For breakfast?"

I shrugged. "I'm on a roll. Beef jerky, now ice cream. I call it the 'Magnolia Grove Maniac' nutrition plan."

As Ronald busied himself with my order, Whit casually leaned against the counter. "We're looking into Walter's murder. Tragic business."

Ronald paused mid-scoop. "Yeah, real tragic. Walter was a good man." He resumed scooping the ice cream and handed the cup to me.

I took a bite, indulging in the creamy white chocolate's velvety sweetness, crunchy cookie dough's satisfying texture, and smooth vanilla's subtle depth. Rich flavors harmonized on my tongue.

Once I swallowed, I said: "We heard you caused quite a scene in Nellie Pritchett's office the other day."

Ronald's cheeks flushed. "Ah, yeah. Bit embarrassing. But I've got full rights to buy that property. The contract was signed and everything."

Whit and I exchanged a glance. "Is that why you were at Walter's place earlier?" I asked. "Looking for the paperwork?"

Ronald nodded a bit too enthusiastically. "Exactly. Just trying to get everything in order, you know?"

"We heard Walter might have been having second thoughts," Whit said carefully.

Ronald put his hands on his hips. "Who told you that? That lying drunk son of his?"

I swirled the ice cream with the plastic spoon. "No. But

speaking of Jesse, he doesn't seem to have nice things to say about you either."

"Walter sold to me because he trusts me. Jesse's just mad because of that. Of course, if I don't find that paperwork that was legally signed, Jesse'll get the property."

I took another little bite of ice cream. "Is that the full story?"

"Sure is."

Whit chimed in. "Ronald, we found the contract. That's how we know Walter was having doubts about selling to you. There was a sticky note attached to it."

Ronald looked like he'd just gotten slapped. "You found it? Where? Can I have it?"

I pointed the plastic spoon at Ronald. "You hadn't signed it yet. And it seems Walter was wavering because you might've had some development plans …"

Ronald sighed, running a hand through his hair. "Alright, alright. Look, I'm not gonna lie. The ice cream business isn't exactly a money maker. A while back, Jesse tossed an idea my way about selling beer, too. Ice cream and beer. Kids come in for the ice cream with their parents, who buy a tasty craft beer."

"Convenient," I said.

Ronald leaned in, lowering his voice. "Yes. I like the idea, so that's what I plan on doing. Use the farm for all my dairy needs and have a little brewery. Then Jesse got all bent out of shape 'cause he thought I stole the idea from him without bringing him on as a business partner." He guffawed. "Can you imagine Jesse as a business partner?"

"No, I can't."

"Anyway, I kept the brewery plans from Walter, figuring he might not be keen on his farm becoming a hub for hops and grain. He'd like to point out there were already enough breweries in town. Plus, I suspected his son's ... enthusiasm for beer might've made him a bit hesitant. But I assured him I wasn't going to sell to any developers or anything like that. And I would still keep things family friendly."

I savored another bite of white chocolate ice cream, its luxurious sweetness at odds with my growing unease. "So, Walter wasn't fully on board. Why have you been insisting that the deal was already done?"

His smile briefly disappeared, then came back. "He *was* going to close the deal."

Whit tapped his fingers on the display case. "Did he tell you that?"

"No, but I could tell. Look, we go way back."

I tilted my head. "You go way back, that's how you could tell?"

Ronald nodded with confidence. "Yes, ma'am."

I shifted gears. "Do you know Jesse's girlfriend, Amber?" I watched his reaction carefully.

He started wiping down the spotless counter and chuckled. "Amber Ray? Sure do. Had some business dealings with her daddy."

"Yes, she mentioned you took a shot at him?"

Ronald let out a laugh, shaking his head as he tossed the rag over his shoulder. "Oh, that? It was just a big misunderstanding. See, I was out hunting with my buddy Skeeter and his brother. We were tracking this big ol' buck when suddenly, Russ's dog—Russ is Amber's daddy, by the way—anyhoo, his dog came bounding through the brush. I stumbled, my gun went off, and the bullet ricocheted off a rock, whizzed past a raccoon, bounced off a tin can, and barely grazed Russ's hat. See, he was out there—unbeknownst to me, mind you—down by the river fishin'. Now, that hardly counts as taking a shot at him."

He leaned on the counter. "Between you and me, I think he's been holding a grudge because I took his crush, Lacy Flippen, to homecoming. You see, he was too afraid to ask her himself, and he's never gotten over that."

"Fascinating." I tapped my spoon against the ice cream cup. "Where were you during the festival when Walter was killed?"

"Left early. Wasn't feeling well."

"Can anyone verify that?"

"No. I was by myself that weekend." Ronald straightened up. "Sally, my wife, is on a Caribbean cruise with her mom. Her mom's getting up there in years and always wanted to go on a cruise. Have you ever been? The buffets are something else—midnight chocolate fountains, prime rib every night, and the entertainment! They've got these acting acrobats who—"

"Ronald," I interrupted before we got a full cruise ship brochure. "Focus."

His face fell, and then his expression shifted. "Wait a minute ... you don't think I killed Walter? I would never!"

"We're just trying to cover all the bases." I glanced at Whit. "Any questions for our ice cream entrepreneur?"

Whit nodded. "Just one, Ronald. If the deal with Walter falls through, what's your backup plan?"

Ronald's smile faltered for just a moment before he recovered. "Well, now, I hadn't really thought about that. I suppose I'd have to look at other properties, maybe scale back my plans a bit. But let's not get ahead of ourselves. I'm sure everything will work out just fine."

I finished my ice cream and tossed the cup and spoon into the waste basket. "Oh yeah, one last question. Who do you think stands to gain from Walter's death?"

Again, Ronald wiped down the counter with practiced efficiency. "Not me, that's for sure. It complicates things quite a bit. Hate to say it, but his son Jesse certainly does. And now that I think about it, there is one person who might find a sort of personal satisfaction in Walter's demise."

"Who?" I asked.

"George Baxter."

Whit's expression contorted with confusion. "George Baxter? His Polar Plunge rival?"

Ronald stopped wiping and scrubbed a stubborn smudge with his thumb. "Been playing second fiddle to Walter since grade school when Walt beat him out for the lead role in the first-grade play, 'Chicken Little.'"

Whit chuckled. "That's a long time to hold a grudge."

Ronald nodded. "It goes on like that. In middle school, Walter edged George out for the science fair top prize with that volcano project. In senior year, Walter swooped in and stole George's sweetheart, Becky Thompson. Married her a year later."

Whit let out a soft *hmm.* "Talk about a life-long rivalry."

Ronald leaned in, lowering his voice. "After Becky left to pursue a career in acting, George blamed Walter."

"Hmm. Okay." I held out some cash.

Ronald waved his hand. "On the house."

"Well, thanks for the ice cream and clarification," I said, turning to leave.

"Wait! What about my contract?"

"I think it'll be on hold for now …"

CHAPTER 8

Whit and I stepped out of Sweet Scoops, the electric bell chiming behind us. The crisp winter air bit at my cheeks. Whit zipped up his jacket, his breath forming little clouds in the cold.

"Well, that was … interesting." I tucked my hands into my pockets. "What do you think about all that?"

"Parker, I don't know what to make of it. In my humble opinion, Ronald bending the truth about Walter signing over the farm to him, making like it was a done deal, was enough to make me wonder."

"Yeah. But so far, we don't have anything solid that gets Lauren off the hook. It's not looking good for her case." I started walking toward Catch You Latte.

Whit nodded, falling into step beside me. "What do you think about talking to George? Get his story and perspective. His gym's just down at the end of Main."

"Might as well walk off some of that ice cream guilt."

We strolled down the sidewalk, our footsteps crunching

on the salt. Whit broke the comfortable silence. "Let's just walk this through ... Say Walter's rival, George, did it. You really think he would murder Walter over a first-grade play and such?"

"You'd be surprised what people are capable of when pride's on the line. Reminds me of an episode I did titled, 'Playground to Prison: When Childhood Grudges Turn Deadly.' This one guy in Idaho held on to a dodgeball grudge for thirty years before he snapped."

Whit's eyebrows shot up. "Seriously?"

"Yep. Let's just say his victim should've dodged a little quicker that time."

We rounded the corner, and my eyes landed on the door of a brick building, where "Baxter's Blue Ridge Boot-camp" was plastered in neon-green letters, complete with a cartoon boot camp instructor yelling, "Drop and give me twenty!"

"Subtle, George isn't," I muttered.

Inside, the boutique gym's rustic-chic decor blended with the harsh realities of CrossFit training. Ropes, tires, and iron weights awaited the brave.

George, with tight-cropped silver curls, fit and muscular in his seventies, towered over a woman with a shocking white globe of permed hair who had to be pushing ninety. "That's it, Mrs. Phelps! Feel the burn in those glutes!"

Mrs. Phelps, bless her heart, was doing squats with more vigor than I could muster on my best day.

George spotted us and waved. "Hey, Whit! Hey, Parker! Y'all come on in! Just finishing up here with Mrs. Phelps."

He turned back to his elderly client. "Remember, ice those knees and take your glucosamine. Same time next week?"

Mrs. Phelps nodded, patting George's arm. "You bet your bippy, sonny. These old bones ain't quittin' yet!"

As she passed us, she winked and said, "If I can do squats, you young'uns can too!"

Whit chuckled, and I smiled.

George beamed, shaking his head. "That Phelps sure is a spitfire. Might outlive us all!"

He made his way to the counter, his grin still in place. "So, what brings you two to my humble sweat palace? Looking to get in shape for swimsuit season?"

"It's January, George," I said.

"Ain't no better time to start!" George exclaimed. "You know, Whit, I've got just the thing for you—my Magnolia Muscle program. Two-for-one special, and I'll throw in a free barre class for Parker here."

Whit side-eyed me. "Barre class?"

George nodded. "Yes, ma'am! Best way to improve flexibility. My wife swears by it. You oughta join us, Parker."

I smiled. "I'll think about it, George."

George reached under the counter. "How about a protein bar? All-natural ingredients, no added sugar."

"I'll pass," Whit said.

"I'll take one." I reached out for the bar.

George went into a little spiel. "The Baxter's Better Bites line is my newest venture. Local honey from a Magnolia Grove apiary and a secret blend of nuts, seeds and pea protein."

Beef jerky, ice cream, and now, a protein bar. All the major food groups. I figured, why not keep my newfound "Magnolia Maniac" nutrition plan going strong?

I unwrapped the bar and took a bite, surprised by the pleasant flavor. "This isn't bad, George. Nutty with a hint of cinnamon."

George burst into a smile. "Spot on! Glad you like it! Been honing the recipe for years."

I took another bite before steering the conversation back to the real reason for our visit. "George, we're here to talk about Walter Carr."

The jovial atmosphere shifted, George's smile fading. "Such a shame. Can't imagine. What do you want to know?"

"You two had quite the rivalry," Whit said.

George's face turned serious. "Look, Whit, I know what you're fishing for, but I had nothing to do with Walter's death. Sure, we were competitive, but we were friends too."

I thought about Ronald's gossip. "'Chicken Little' in first grade to Becky in high school. Not still bitter about Becky, are you?"

George let out a hearty laugh. "Oh, come now. Becky and I were already on the outs when she and Walter got together. Heck, I was in their wedding, for Pete's sake." He shook his head, a wry smirk on his face. "Let me guess—someone whose name rhymes with Donald told you I blamed Walter for her skipping town?"

I tilted my head, surprised by his perceptiveness.

George continued. "That's a load of hogwash. That man's got more tall tales than a library full of books. Becky had always wanted to become an actress and move to Tinsel Town … Some folks in this town just can't let old stories die."

He leaned in, lowering his voice. "If anyone had a grudge, it was probably Ronald. He had a thing for Becky back in the day, but that's ancient history."

Hmm. Funny, Ronald hadn't mentioned that part of the story … "So, you're saying there was no bad blood between you and Walter?"

George shook his head firmly. "None whatsoever. Sure, we ribbed each other about the Polar Plunge and whatnot, but it was all in good fun. Kept us both young, you know?"

"Speaking of the Polar Plunge, where were you right before Walter was found?"

"I was down at the lake, doin' my calisthenics, getting ready for the plunge. Right before that, I was talking to Nellie, joking for her to get ready to hand that trophy to me."

"Notice anything out of the ordinary?" I watched his face carefully.

George scratched his chin, thinking. "Besides Walter not being the first one there to psych everyone else out? Naw." He paused, then added, "Though I was a bit surprised to see Jules Winston there. She ain't ever done the plunge before. Good for her, though! I love seeing my clients stretch their comfort zone!"

I recalled Hazel's enthusiasm at seeing her hero—Jules—getting ready for the event.

"One more thing, George … Who do you think might've shot Walter?"

George shook his head. "No idea ... he was a decent man that might've been a bit ornery and set in his ways, but I ain't got a clue."

I finished the last bite of the protein bar, surprisingly satisfied. "Thanks for your time, George. And for the snack."

"Anytime, Parker. Y'all come back now, you hear?" He reached under the counter and pulled out two cards. "Here's a couple of free passes. Never hurts to stay in shape."

Whit and I took the cards and thanked him.

We stepped outside, where the air was chilly despite the afternoon sun.

"What are you thinking?" Whit asked.

"I'm thinking George had nothing to do with any of this and it's time to get back to the cafe. I hope Hazel hasn't blown the place up."

"I'm reckoning she's holding her own. I best get back to work myself. You know Delacroix. His grand vision is turning those rumrunning tunnels into a museum."

I thought about the maze of brick passageways beneath the town. "That's actually not a bad idea."

Whit gave me a quick peck on the cheek before heading to his car. I watched him walk away, a grin playing at my lips. Who'd have thought the town historian would turn out to be my partner in both crime-solving and romance? The way his eyes crinkled when he laughed, how he could turn even the driest historical fact into something fascinating—I found myself growing more attached with each passing day.

I started the short walk to my cafe, passing by Feta & Friends as quickly as possible to avoid Lauren. The morning sun tried its best to warm the crisp winter air. I'd barely made it past the shop when a chipper voice called out behind me.

"Parker! Wait up!"

Jules Winston strode toward me, her confident demeanor matched by her sleek, sophisticated look. She wore a tailored winter coat in camel cashmere and a matching knit cap, carrying a stylish gym bag that probably cost more than my monthly coffee bean shipment.

"I'm glad I caught you ..."

"Hey, Jules. How's it going?"

"I am well. Heading to George's for a workout. His CrossFit classes are unbeatable—nothing like his old-school, no-nonsense style to keep you on your toes. Do you work out there?"

I gestured toward the cafe. "My workout routine consists of lifting coffee mugs and wiping down the kitchen after Hazel's baking rampages."

Jules nodded and laughed. "Gotcha. If you ever feel like stepping up your game, George's is the place to go."

"I'm sure it is. Maybe I'll give it a shot. I was just there, and George gave me a free pass."

"Oh? What were you doing there if not working out?"

"Just some questions for Lauren's case."

"Ahh, yes. How's that going?"

"I can't comment on an ongoing investigation," I said carefully.

Jules nodded understandingly. "Of course. I just have a hard time believing Lauren would do such a thing."

"Actually, can I ask you something?"

"Sure, fire away."

"Aside from their petty differences, do you know of any reason Lauren would kill Walter?"

Jules's expression turned thoughtful. "Full disclosure: I was interested in buying Walter's farm, but he backed out. When I asked him why, he said—and I quote—'You're tied to that money-grubbing city slicker who's done me and others wrong.' He was referring to Lauren. No skin off my back, though; business is business. It happens all the time. But when I first casually mentioned that exchange to Lauren, her reaction was ... telling."

"Telling?"

"I would say she was apoplectic." Jules paused, looking slightly uncomfortable. "I shouldn't jump to conclusions ... You'll clear her name, won't you?"

My expression remained neutral, but my tone hinted at a subtle shift. "We'll see."

Jules's eyes narrowed slightly, as though she were processing my ambiguity. Then she smiled, a wolfish gleam in her eye. "Anyway, I'm glad I caught you, because I've been thinking about our previous conversation. I'm willing to make a very attractive offer."

"Oh?"

"Can we discuss it over dinner tonight? My treat, of course. I have some ideas I think you'll find ... irresistible."

I hesitated, then surrendered to my curiosity. "Alright, Jules, you've whetted my appetite. Can't hurt to talk."

"Excellent. Let's say 7 PM at The Old Courthouse Grill. I'll make the reservations."

I nodded, trying not to let my surprise show. The Old Courthouse Grill was the fanciest restaurant in town and was located in Magnolia Grove's former historic courthouse building. Fully renovated, of course.

"Sounds great. I'll see you then."

As Jules sashayed away, I stood rooted to the sidewalk, my mind whirling. The Old Courthouse Grill? Thank goodness Jules was paying; if it were up to me, I'd be asking for a payment plan by the time the bread arrived.

Between investigating Walter's murder, running the cafe and now Jules's expansion proposal, my plate was piled higher than one of Hazel's infamous triple-layer mocha cakes. Speaking of Hazel—I checked the time and winced. I'd left her alone in the cafe for over two hours. While her enthusiasm for the job knew no bounds, her talent for chaos was equally limitless. With any luck, she'd managed to keep both the coffee flowing and the kitchen standing.

The case could wait. My theories about Lauren's innocence, Jesse's strange behavior and Jules's business propositions would still be there after I made sure my assistant hadn't turned my kitchen into a disaster zone.

CHAPTER 9

The afternoon lull settled over Catch You Latte like a warm blanket. Earlier, I'd managed to make it back just before the lunch crowd descended, but I needn't have worried. Hazel had handled the morning rush with surprising competence while I was out sleuthing around town. Even now, hours later, the kitchen still looked marginally less destroyed than usual—a minor miracle in the grand scheme of Hazel's baking chaos.

"Now that the rush is over, tell me … how'd it go?" Hazel was arranging a new batch of fresh-baked cookies in the display case next to some pre-cut slices of cheesecake. "Did Jesse do it? Or was it Lauren? Ooh, or maybe Ethan?" Her mint-colored bob swung with each theory.

"Slow down there, Nancy Drew." I filled her in on the morning's events—Jesse's brand-new truck and suspicious memory gaps about the festival, Ronald's false claims about Walter signing over the farm and George's seeming lack of murderous rivalry.

Hazel straightened up, nearly knocking over the cookie display she'd just arranged. "Wow, this is better than 'Shelf Life and Death'—that new true-crime podcast about the librarian who—"

"Maybe I should compare notes with Colton," I said, cutting off what would surely be a detailed plot synopsis. "See what the *official* investigation has turned up."

I unplugged my phone from the wall charger and tapped "Magnolia Grove's Finest"—my label for the sheriff's department. After a few rings, a familiar, unenthused voice answered. "Magnolia Grove Sheriff's Office."

"Hi, Leigh Ann. It's Parker Hayes. Is Deputy Colton available?"

I could practically hear her eyes rolling through the phone. The steady *tap-tap-tap* of her fingers on what I assumed was her ever-present smartphone provided a rhythmic backdrop to her sigh. "Hold on."

A moment later, Colton's calm voice came on the line. "Hayes? What's going on?"

"Deputy, I was hoping we could compare notes on the Walter Carr case. I've been hired by Lauren's attorney, Roger Buzzard, to—"

"Save it, Hayes." Colton cut me off. "You might as well drop this one. We've got Lauren dead to rights. She killed Walter Carr."

I blinked, taken aback. "What? Do you have new evidence?"

"Sure do. We searched her condo and found a box of bullets that match the caliber of the murder weapon—right inside a potted plant in her living room. Plus, we found a strand of gray hair on her coat, likely Walter's. It's been sent to the lab, and once the results come back, it's a done deal. This case is wrapped up tighter than a Mason jar of peach preserves."

I sat down on the stool behind the counter. "Don't you think finding that evidence was a bit convenient?"

"Parker, not everything is a conspiracy. Sometimes the answer's as clear as day."

I was speechless, which, as you know, is a rare occurrence.

Colton's tone shifted to courteous. "Thank you again for looking into the matter, Parker. Take care now."

The line went silent.

I turned to Hazel, my expression grim. "Looks like Lauren's goose is cooked." I filled her in on what Colton had told me—the bullets hidden in the potted plant, the gray hair on Lauren's coat …

Hazel stopped slicing into the salted caramel cheesecake. "But why would Lauren keep evidence in her own house? That's like, Criminal Behavior 101—don't keep murder stuff at home!"

"Either way, Colton sounded pretty sure he has irrefutable evidence. Things aren't looking good for our cheese entrepreneur. Honestly, Hazel, I'm not so sure she *didn't* do it. She was acting peculiar when I questioned her earlier."

"But she's too smart to be messy," Hazel said.

"I agree, but there's not much more I can do. Except call Buzzard to let him know I'm done."

Hazel went back to cutting slices of cheesecake and

placing them in the display case. The aroma of coffee and sugary sweets swirled around me, a comforting presence in the face of the uncomfortable task ahead.

With a deep breath, I steeled myself and dialed Roger Buzzard's number. The phone rang twice before his nasally voice crackled through the speaker.

"Buzzard here."

"Roger, it's Parker Hayes."

"Ah, Miss Hayes. Progress report on our little predicament, I hope?"

I traced abstract patterns on the counter. "Actually, I'm calling to tell you I'm off the case."

A moment of silence hung between us. Then, he said, "Is it because of the new evidence?"

"Yep."

Buzzard guffawed. "The bullets and the hair on her coat, like the weapon in her purse, were planted."

I bit back a snarky pun about planted evidence hidden in a plant. "Then why won't Lauren give her alibi? It's not exactly helping her case."

Buzzard's sigh crackled through the phone. "She has her reasons."

"Well, those reasons better be good enough for a jury," I muttered. "Look, Roger, I've done what I can. The evidence is stacked against her."

"I see," Buzzard said, his voice cooling. "Well, thank you for your … efforts, Miss Hayes. I shall mail you a check for services rendered."

"No need, Roger. If you feel inclined to do so, donate it to a good cause. And good luck, you're gonna need it." I hung up before he could respond.

Hazel looked up from the display case. "You think Buzzard still believes Lauren's innocent?"

"As long as she's paying him, he'll believe whatever she says."

"Parker!" Hazel nearly dropped a chocolate chip cookie. "That's kind of harsh."

I softened. "You're right. I shouldn't be like that. Maybe Buzzard genuinely thinks it's a frame job."

"What if he's right?" Hazel carefully repositioned the cookie on the display shelf.

"If he is, then she needs to provide a solid alibi." I stood up to make us some Minted Mayhem Lattes.

Hazel grabbed a couple of mugs and set them next to the espresso machine. "That evidence did seem awfully convenient, though. Almost too perfect."

I tamped down the coffee grounds into the portafilter. "Yeah, I guess. But convenient or not, evidence doesn't lie. And Lauren's silence isn't helping her case."

"True." Hazel sighed, handing me the peppermint syrup.

The bell above the door chimed, and in walked Clyde, with Major trotting happily at his heels. The little mutt's tail wagged furiously at the sight of me. Clyde carried one of his famous pecan pies in his free hand.

"Hey there, Parker," Clyde called out, his trademark white-bearded grin in place. "Got a favor to ask." He walked to the counter and set down the pie. The warm scent of sugary caramelized pecans baked in homemade pie crust enveloped me.

I let Hazel finish up the lattes and went around the

counter to give Major a good ear scratch. "What's up, guys? What's with the pie?"

"I have a favor to ask ..."

"Ah, so you come bearing goods ..."

"I need to head out of town for a few days. My sister's having some trouble with her well pump, and she's stubborn as a mule about asking for help."

I stood up. "Let me guess. You need someone to dog-sit? You didn't need to bribe me, but I'm not going to turn down your heavenly pecan pie."

Clyde's grin widened. "She's allergic to dogs. Plus, this little rascal misses you."

I looked down at Major, who was now doing his best "sad puppy" impression. "Oh, alright," I teased. "How can I resist that face? We'll have a grand old time, won't we, Major?"

Major let out an enthusiastic yip, his entire backside wagging.

Clyde handed me Major's leash. "Thanks, Parker. You're a lifesaver. My sister's in the hills, so Pickler let me borrow his F-150. So if you need a vehicle ..." He handed me the keys to Bertha, his vintage station wagon.

"You're the best!"

Clyde studied me for a moment, always tuned in when something was off. "Everything else okay?"

"This Lauren Yancey case. Something's off about it. Part of me thinks she's guilty, another doesn't."

Clyde scrunched his bushy white eyebrows. "Sometimes the ones who seem guilty are innocent, and the ones who seem innocent are guilty."

I smirked. "Who said that?"

Clyde chuckled. "I thought you did! … Anyhoo, Parker, it's solvable. And I know you'll be the one to do it."

"Thanks, Clyde. But I'm off the case."

"Mm-hmm …"

Hazel piped up, "Hey, Clyde, want some coffee for the road?"

"Well, now that you mention it, I've been hankering to try that new Mint Mayhem *dealymajig* everyone's talking about."

"Coming right up!" Hazel chirped, bustling to finish the two lattes we'd already started.

"Mint Mayhem *dealymajig*?" I echoed, amused.

Clyde snickered. "Isn't that what you youngsters are saying?"

"Right before we dance the Jitterbug," I joked.

Hazel handed Clyde a to-go cup. "Drive safe, Clyde."

With a salute, Clyde left the cafe.

I turned to Major. "Ready for a walk, furball?"

Major's excited bark was all the answer I needed. I put on my peacoat.

"Going to take Major for a walk, clear my head a bit," I told Hazel.

She handed me a Mint Mayhem in a to-go cup. "I promise not to burn the place down while you're gone. Probably."

She pulled out the bag of Crazy Carl's Jerky from under the counter where I'd stashed it. "Here, Major, best jerky in three counties!" She tore off a piece and popped it in her mouth, then offered a piece to Major, who took it with gentlemanly delicacy.

"You actually like that leather masquerading as food?" I watched in amazement as she happily chewed away.

"Are you kidding? My brother swears by Crazy Carl's. Says it builds character." She gave Major another piece, which he accepted with considerably less restraint than the first.

"Well, at least someone's getting enjoyment out of it." I shook my head at their shared enthusiasm. "Just don't blame me when your jaw locks up."

Outside, the crisp air nipped at my cheeks as Major, his jerky already devoured, and I strolled through town. Though the case was closed, my mind wandered back to its twists and turns. Old habits died hard.

"Okay, Major, let's think this through," I mused aloud. "Hypothetically speaking, if there's a slim chance Lauren's innocent, who else had a motive?"

Major sniffed at a fire hydrant, clearly riveted by my detective work.

"Ronald Sweetwater wanted that farm badly. Maybe badly enough to kill?" I pondered as Major left his mark on the hydrant. "Then there's Jesse Carr, angry that his dad was going to sell off what he felt was rightfully his inheritance. And George Baxter had that long-standing rivalry ..."

Major suddenly lunged forward, nearly yanking my arm out of its socket as he chased a squirrel.

"Whoa, easy there, Scooby Clue," I laughed, regaining my balance. "I don't think the squirrel did it."

As we rounded a corner, I nearly collided with a familiar face.

Ethan, cheese-making maestro, stood shivering in his T-shirt, rubbing his arms to warm himself. The graphic on his shirt read, "Cheese Aficionado." His eyes darted nervously as he exclaimed, "Parker! I need to tell you something."

"What's going on?" I asked.

He glanced around before kneeling down to scratch Major behind the ears. "I saw something weird at the cheese shop."

My interest stirred. "Oh yeah?"

Ethan stood back up, dusting off his knees. "I was rearranging the display—I'm trying to perfect a geometric mosaic with our brie and blue cheese—when I accidentally knocked over Sophia's bag."

He paused, collecting his thoughts. "Anyway, a bunch of stuff fell out. One of the items was a burner phone."

"Sophia has a burner phone ... okay, and?"

"And ... I saw a sent text on it," Ethan said.

"Looks like I'm not the only 'nosey parker.'"

"Whatever. The text said: '*This goes deeper than you think. Stay out of it, coffee girl. This isn't amateur hour!* ' I'm assuming it was sent to you." Ethan's eyes locked onto mine.

I thought about the text I'd received earlier with those exact words. What were the odds?

"Are you absolutely sure that this was Sophia's burner phone?"

He nodded vigorously. "Positive. What do you think it means?"

I patted his shoulder. "I'm not sure, but I can promise I'll find out. Thanks, Ethan."

"Cool. I better go. I'm freezing."

As Ethan hurried off, I looked down at Major, who tilted his head curiously.

"Well, buddy, looks like we've got a question that needs to be answered."

Major's tail wagged in response. Whether he understood or not, it was clear—this case might not be over.

I tugged gently on Major's leash, and we continued toward the town square. My mind was ignited with questions. What was Sophia's angle? Why send an anonymous text? I pulled out my phone, thumbs hovering over the screen, and I started typing a text response to the unknown number.

Hi there, Sophia [waving hand emoji]. Coffee girl here. Wanna come by the cafe for a [coffee cup emoji] and chat about why you're sending me secret messages?

I hit send, half-expecting it to remain unread, but the response came almost immediately:

I can explain everything ...

Well, butter my biscuit and call me intrigued. Looked like Sophia had some 'splainin' to do, and I was all ears.

"Alright, Major ... Let's head back to the cafe. I have a feeling things are about to get interesting."

Major yipped in agreement as we turned toward Catch You Latte, ready to unravel another layer of this cheesy mystery.

I TOOK Major to my upstairs apartment and left him snug in his little bed, his tail thumping contentedly against the cushion. "Be good, buddy. I'll be back soon," I said before heading back down to the cafe.

The bell above the cafe door jangled, and Sophia rushed in. Her ponytail was loose and disheveled, with strands of hair dangling in disarray. Her gaze darted nervously around the place as she approached the counter.

"Parker," she said breathlessly.

I nodded toward the kitchen. "Let's talk in my 'office.'" I turned to Hazel, who was wiping down the counter, trying to pretend like she wasn't completely intrigued by this new development. "Hazel, the ship is yours again."

She gave me a salute. "Aye aye, captain!"

Sophia followed me to the kitchen, which was again a disaster zone thanks to Hazel's mad genius. I pointed toward a folding table and two chairs in the alcove, my makeshift workspace. We sat down, the scent of baked cookies and cheesecakes saturating the air.

I leaned back in my chair. "My apologies for the mess. But let's get to the real matter. Why did you send an anonymous text telling me to drop the case?"

Sophia's nervousness melted away, replaced by a glint of … pride? "As you know, I was a business and psych major in college. I knew telling you to back away and insulting you would only motivate you to solve the case. I got worried when you told Lauren you were done. Sorry for the harsh words."

I jerked forward, eyeballing her. "So you were using reverse psychology on me?"

She nodded. "It worked."

"Hmmph."

"You're driven by challenges, Parker. You have a strong sense of justice, but you also enjoy the thrill of solving puzzles. I would've loved to design an escape room just for you!" Her excitement was building. "And your snarky and sometimes cocky exterior masks a deep empathy for others and a bit of an insecurity. Also, unrelated, you have an obsession with coffee that borders on pathological."

I blinked, impressed by her analysis despite myself. "Okay, Dr. Freud, you've made your point. But why the cloak-and-dagger routine?"

Sophia's excitement faded. "Because Lauren *is* innocent. And I needed your help to prove it. When you stormed out of the shop, I got desperate."

I folded my arms across my chest and leaned back. "I'm listening."

Sophia took a deep breath, her hands clasped tightly, resting on the table. "Lauren has an alibi for the time of Walter's murder, but she's too afraid to come forward with it."

"Why? What could be so damning that she'd rather be charged with murder?"

Sophia glanced around as if checking for eavesdroppers in my kitchen. "Lauren's 'errand' that day? Well … she went to Walter's dairy farm to let Bessie out."

I cocked my head, sure I'd misheard. "Bessie? Walter's prize cow?"

Sophia exhaled, her expression dead serious. "Lauren was convinced Walter was the one who defaced the banner for our booth. She wanted revenge."

"So she committed bovine liberation? A second time?" I couldn't keep the incredulity out of my voice. "That's her big secret?"

"First of all, she didn't let Bessie out that first time. Walter just accused her of it."

"Okay ..."

"There's more," Sophia continued, her voice dropping to a whisper. "She also accidentally knocked over the statue of the town founder, Magnolia Mike. She was in a hurry to get back to the festival and ran into it with her car. She panicked, quickly parked and ran back to the festival, making like nothing happened. By that time, everyone was already gathering around Walter's body. So she couldn't have done it."

I stared off at the messy kitchen, processing this information. This whole scenario was ridiculous.

I pinched the bridge of my nose. "Let me get this straight. Lauren Yancey, artisanal cheese maven and self-proclaimed sophisticate, orchestrated a cow jailbreak as revenge for a vandalized sign, then accidentally toppled a statue?"

"Yes."

I furrowed my brow, thinking it through. "But this is her alibi. She couldn't have killed Walter if she was off liberating Bessie and crashing into statues."

Sophia shook her head. "I understand, but Lauren doesn't see it that way. She thinks the optics are all wrong.

In her mind, her business would go down the tubes if she were outed for releasing Bessie—the town loves that cow. But she's especially worried about being held responsible for toppling the statue."

I stared at Sophia, astonished. "So she's keeping quiet because she thinks admitting to the cow prank and the statue accident would ruin her business?"

Sophia nodded solemnly.

"That's worse than having a murder charge?" My voice rose in disbelief and befuddlement.

Sophia's eyes lit up, that psychology-major gleam returning. "Perhaps, yes. Lauren's mind works in … unique ways. She might even subconsciously think that being wrongfully accused of murder, then vindicated down the line, would be good for business. Strangely brilliant, huh?"

I stared at Sophia, my jaw practically on the floor. "Or she's totally insane!"

"Well," Sophia mused, tapping her chin thoughtfully, "from a psychological standpoint, Lauren exhibits narcissistic tendencies with a dash of imposter syndrome. She's constantly seeking validation while simultaneously fearing exposure as a fraud. This combination can lead to some … let's say, questionable decision-making. But that's usually the case with visionary geniuses."

I shook my head. "Great. So we're dealing with a cheese business mastermind who thinks being a murder suspect is good PR … Just when I thought this case couldn't get any weirder."

"Welcome to the fascinating world of Lauren Yancey's mind," Sophia said with a wry smile.

"Remind me to stick to coffee and stay out of cheese," I muttered. "Alright, let's go talk to our resident visionary genius. Something tells me this conversation is going to be a real *gouda* time."

Sophia looked perplexed, then smiled. "Ahh, I get it. A cheese pun. Humorous. Anyway, we'll have to head to her townhome. After Roger Buzzard called her, she closed the shop."

As we headed for the door, I wondered what other surprises this case had in store. One thing was certain—in Magnolia Grove, nothing was ever as simple as it seemed.

CHAPTER 10

The setting sun cast long shadows across Main Street as Sophia and I made our way toward Lauren's condo a few blocks away.

I gazed at the sleek, industrial-chic live-work complex, its modern brick facade exuding sophistication.

"Nice digs," I said.

The building stood out among the charming historical structures, yet seamlessly blended in. To its left sat an old feed shop, reminiscent of the 1800s, and to its right, a small brewery, cleverly retro-fitted from a former auto shop. The condominium's modern design, with crisp brick and sleek lines, surprisingly complemented the town's quaint atmosphere. A hip Thai restaurant on the ground floor filled the air with the scents of spice and coconut.

This development was a key part of Jackson Beauregard's visionary "grand plan" to revitalize Magnolia Grove's older districts.

His other project in the works—which included the old

building that housed Maggie's Boutique--had yet to get past the planning phase. The multi-use development had faced a series of hurdles and setbacks since I had moved to town. One thing I'd come to learn about Magnolia Grove was that any change, no matter how small, divided the town right down the middle. Half the people loved new things like this swanky complex, while the other half clung to tradition like it was the last life raft on the Titanic. Progress versus preservation—the eternal small-town tug-of-war.

We entered the small lobby, surprisingly cozy for such a modern space. Gotta hand it to Jackson, he kept things classy. The elevator dinged open, and we stepped inside.

Sophia pressed the button. "Lauren's on the third floor."

I leaned against the elevator wall, crossing my arms. "So, does Lauren's condo come with a separate cheese cave, or is that extra?"

"No, she wouldn't ... oh, you're joking," Sophia realized, then smiled. For someone skilled in the brains department, she sure didn't catch humorous nuances.

The doors opened, revealing a hallway that looked more like a boutique hotel than an apartment complex.

We stopped in front of Lauren's door. I took a deep breath, steadying myself for the confrontation ahead. "Ready to face the big cheese?"

Sophia nodded. "I texted her to let her know we were coming." She knocked on the door.

The muffled sound of heels clicking on hardwood approached. The door swung open, revealing Lauren. Her eyes were puffy and red-rimmed, though she quickly composed herself, trying to hide any evidence of tears.

"I thought you were off the case." Lauren's voice was slightly hoarse.

"Well … I changed my mind. Again."

She hesitated for a moment, then stepped aside. "Come in."

Lauren's condo was a study in modern minimalism with a touch of industrial charm. Sleek furniture contrasted with exposed brick walls, while artisanal cheese boards hung like artwork.

My nose twitched. Did I smell beer?

Lauren gestured to the police evidence card on her coffee table. "They confiscated my Gucci. That coat is worth more than a monthly mortgage payment. I wasn't even wearing it the day Walter was shot." Her expression turned sour. "And look." She pointed to the potted plant by the window. "That's where they 'found' the bullets. Bullets!" Lauren scoffed, rolling her eyes. "I wouldn't know a .38 from a .22 if I had a diagram. And if I did know about this stuff, don't you think I'd be clever enough to hide bullets somewhere better?"

"I know your alibi," I said flatly.

Lauren's head whipped toward me, then Sophia, eyes flashing.

Sophia cried out, "I'm sorry, Lauren. I just don't want you to go to prison."

I raised my hands. "Calm down, everybody. Lauren, you need to tell Colton the truth."

Lauren's shoulders slumped. "They'll railroad me like they always do. The outsider who came to shake things up. It's the perfect scapegoat story."

Oh, the martyrdom … "Well, not to offer unsolicited advice, but have you considered being a bit kinder to the locals?"

"What's that have to do with anything?"

"Never mind."

That faint scent of stale beer tickled my nose again. I scanned the room, spotting only an empty wine glass on the side table. "Have you been drinking beer?"

She wrinkled her nose in distaste. "Please, beer? All those carbs? Just a glass of Pinot Noir."

"I smell beer in here," I insisted.

Lauren's expression changed to thoughtful. "Now that you mention it, I thought I caught a whiff earlier. Must be from that microbrewery next door."

I knew better. This scent was coming from inside her place. My notoriously keen sense of smell had proven both a blessing and a curse in my life.

I began to circle the room, following the scent. As I walked, my shoe stuck slightly to the hardwood floor. I lifted my foot, noticing the sticky patch.

"Lauren, did you spill something here?" I pointed to the spot.

"No."

I dropped to my hands and knees, taking a deep sniff. Sure enough: beer.

I stood, eyes locked on the planter, and began walking

toward it. The floor crunched beneath my feet. I knelt to investigate, finding tiny yellow shards—potato chip fragments.

"Lauren, I'm guessing you don't snack on potato chips?"

Her response dripped with sarcasm. "Wow, your detective skills are staggering."

I straightened up, my mind forming a picture. "Looks like we have two possibilities: either Deputy Colton had an impromptu lunchtime happy hour while searching your place, or I've got a pretty good idea who's trying to frame you."

Lauren put her hands on her hips. "Who?"

"I'd rather not say yet."

Sophia perked up. "Does this mean you can prove Lauren's innocence?"

I gave them my best serious look. "For that to happen, Lauren, you'll need to provide Colton with your alibi. Because when the hair sample results come back—likely matching Walter's—they'll send you right to the slammer."

Lauren's expression turned to resignation. "Fine. I'll call Buzzard and set it up." She glanced at Sophia. "Arrange a meeting with Jules. We need to get ahead of the PR fallout."

I had to hand it to Lauren: even with a murder charge hanging over her head, her mind was on business. I wasn't sure if I should admire her resilience or question her emotional detachment.

~

I LEFT LAUREN'S CONDO. The scent of beer and those telltale potato chip crumbs had given me a solid lead, but I wasn't quite ready to confront my suspect head-on just yet. First, I needed more intel from someone close to him.

My boots clomped against the sidewalk as I turned off Main Street onto Vance Street. Nestled between an optometrist's office and an insurance agency, Amber's Hair Affairs occupied an old brick building, its charm subtly revealed by the worn stone façade. A hand-painted sidewalk sign, adorned with colorful graphics and a dash of sass, beckoned passersby: "Free Trim with Color Service—Because You're Worth It (Duh)."

As I pushed open the door, a soft chime above it announced my arrival. Inside, the salon was a vibrant mashup of vintage flair and eclectic whimsy. A 1950s-era beauty parlor chair sat alongside a modern, neon-lit mirror. Retro posters and vinyl records adorned the walls, alongside quirky signs:

"I'm Not Late, I'm Just Fashionably Delayed"

"Hair Goals *Are* Life Goals"

"Warning: Our Stylists May Convincingly Argue You Need Bangs"

The air was thick with the scent of lavender, hairspray, and freshly brewed coffee. Vintage hairdryers hung from the ceiling, while a nearby shelf displayed Amber's collection of quirky trinkets—a vintage gumball machine, a taxidermied owl wearing an updo, and a "World's Okayest Hairstylist" mug. Softly spinning on a classic record player, Dolly Parton's iconic voice streamed through the salon, crooning "Jolene." The warm crackle of static and gentle pop of the needle added to the cozy ambiance, transporting me to a bygone era.

Amber's cheerful voice rang out from behind a shampoo station. "Parker! Be right with ya!"

I settled into one of the pink waiting chairs, scanning the coffee table for a distraction from my impending interrogation. My eyes landed on a dog-eared "Starlet Scoop" magazine featuring the outrageous headline: "Alien Baby Bump: The Shocking Truth!" I chuckled and began flipping through the pages.

Amber emerged from behind the shampoo station, leading a lady, her silver hair styled to perfection. The customer patted her coiffure as she settled into Amber's styling chair. Amber herself looked like a completely different person from the woman I'd met at Jesse's trailer. Her amber waves were expertly styled, framing her face. She wore a chic black salon smock that accentuated her figure, and her makeup was flawless—a far cry from the messy top knot and oversized T-shirt I'd seen in the morning when we were at Jesse's. Her manicured hands deftly adjusted the older woman's hair, adding a final spritz of hairspray.

The woman gazed at her reflection and said, "Back to our previous conversation ... Can you believe Roger Buzzard is representing that murderer? And Jules Winston ... I knew her daddy—good man. Why in heaven's name would she stay in business with the likes of Lauren Yancey?"

Amber smiled warmly, smoothing a few stray hairs.

"Well, Mrs. Bootwright, you know what they say—don't judge a book by its cover."

"I suppose," the lady, Mrs. Bootwright, sighed. "Still, it's a right shame what's happening to our little town."

Amber beamed, holding up a mirror. "There we go, Mrs. Bootwright. All done and looking fabulous!"

Mrs. Bootwright admired her reflection, then tottered with Amber to the register. She pulled out her embroidered wallet and asked, "How much is it, sweetie?"

"Today's total for you is $45," Amber replied.

Mrs. Bootwright's eyes widened. "Lord have mercy, I remember when a haircut was $25!"

Amber laughed. "Well, Mrs. Bootwright, we've got inflation, but we've also got the best hair-care services in town!"

Mrs. Bootwright chuckled, handing over her payment. Cash, of course. "I reckon that's true." She exited the salon, still muttering about Magnolia Grove's decline.

Amber turned to me, her eyes sparkling. "Well, aren't you quite fortuitous? My four-thirty just canceled."

"Oh, I don't need a haircut," I started to protest.

Amber waved off my objection. "Nonsense, sweetie! I insist. Those ends are crying out for some TLC."

I opened my mouth to argue, but Amber was already steering me toward the shampoo station.

"I promise you'll feel like a new woman when I'm done with you."

My resolve crumbled. Maybe a little pampering wouldn't hurt—and it might loosen Amber's tongue about Jesse.

"Alright," I conceded. "Work your magic."

I settled into the shampoo chair, and Amber's skilled fingers began massaging my scalp, working out the tension with gentle circular motions.

"So, how's your day been?" Amber asked, her voice warm and inviting.

"Not too shabby," I replied, feeling my muscles relax. "How about you?"

Amber beamed. "Busy as a bee in a bonnet but wouldn't have it any other way!" She winked, her pretty green eyes sparkling with curiosity. "Hey, you're from the big city, right? And I heard you had a podcast or something?"

"Yes, I was a city slicker for many years. *Criminally Yours*; it was a true-crime podcast. I decided to hang it up."

Amber's interest stirred. "No kidding! What on earth brought you to Magnolia Grove?"

"I needed a change." I kept it short, leaving out the complicated details.

Amber nodded sympathetically. "I hear ya. I'm from out of town myself, but not the city. The Outer Banks—specifically, Hatteras. You ever been?"

As Amber expertly worked the shampoo into a rich lather, I thought about the Outer Banks—that chain of barrier islands along North Carolina's coast, over two hundred miles east of Magnolia Grove's foothills.

"Haven't had the chance yet. I hope to soon. Maybe after my parents move here."

Amber's glossy lips curled upward. "They're movin' here? How wonderful! Magnolia Grove sure is growing. Now let me tell you: if you're gonna head to the Outer

Banks, spring is the time to go. Or fall. And if you're ever in Hatteras, try out Billy's Fried Shrimp Shack right off the beach. Billy's my uncle."

"I'll keep that in mind," I said.

As Amber rinsed my hair and applied a nourishing conditioner, she continued. "Loved growing up there, but I had big dreams. Started doing hair in my mama's kitchen when my only clients were Barbie dolls and family pets."

"That's cute. I used to send my dolls out on detective capers," I said, smiling at the memory.

She chuckled, then continued. "Moved to Magnolia Grove when I was eighteen, attended the prestigious Beauty Barn school—yeah, that's really its name! Loved it here, so I stayed. Now look at me! I've got plans to expand, maybe even franchise. Just like my idol Dolly Parton says, 'The way I see it, if you want the rainbow, you gotta put up with the rain.'" Her grin was radiant.

As Amber worked her magic on my hair, Dolly's "9 to 5" played softly in the background. I took the opportunity to bring Jesse into the conversation.

"So, where does Jesse Carr fit into the picture?"

"We've been dating a couple years now. He's fixin' to help on the business side. He's toying around with the idea for me to franchise. Says he's got vision and connections." Amber applied a pineapple-scented mask to my hair.

Jesse Carr had vision and connections? He seemed more like a beer and potato chips guy to me.

"What sort of connections?" I asked.

"I'm not rightly sure, but someone's already fronted him money for some other business he's been doing."

I filed away that information. "How's Jesse been holding up since his dad died?"

Amber's cheerful demeanor dimmed slightly. "Bless his heart, he and his daddy weren't on the best of terms, on account of Jesse's … fondness for cold ones. I'm trying to help him ease back. I personally don't have a taste for alcohol. But he's gone off the deep end since it happened. It's gotten to him."

"Well, it was his father."

Amber sighed, working conditioner through my ends. "You're right about that. He's fixated on that Lauren Yancey, just like half the town. Keeps saying, 'Gotta make sure she's convicted,' like he thinks she'll go free or something."

Or unravel his own possible involvement in his father's murder … I kept that one to myself. Instead, I said, "Death of a loved one can do strange things to a person."

"You got that right!"

Pieces of the puzzle were clicking into place. I hated to deploy my shadier tactics on Amber, so I decided to play it straight. Remember, I was trying to turn over a new leaf. Less shifty tactics and all that.

"Amber, after Whit and I left Jesse's this morning, did he go anywhere?"

Amber's hands paused, her eyelashes fluttering slightly. "Why?"

"Full disclosure, I'm trying to figure out what happened and prove if Lauren is guilty or innocent."

Amber's expression turned somber. "You think Jesse might've had something to do with it?"

I hesitated. "I don't know. It might help to know where he's been today."

Amber's gaze lingered on mine, then she nodded. "Thank you for being honest. That goes a long way in my book. He dropped me off here maybe a half-hour after you and Whit left. Said he had a bunch of business to attend to. He doesn't tell me details, though I think his business went well."

"Why do you say that?"

"He called me after lunch. He seemed lighter than usual. Even mentioned 'things were looking up.' He's gonna pick me up at six and take me out on a proper date to the Old Courthouse! We've never been there before. A bit pricey."

She wasn't wrong about that. And I found it downright suspicious that Jesse could suddenly afford a dinner there, not to mention the brand-new Silverado he was cruising around in. I was curious about this new "business" Jesse was involved in.

Amber turned on the warm water. "Alright, sugar, let's rinse you out and get you trimmed and styled. You're gonna look fabulous!"

After she rinsed out the conditioner, we moved over to the styling chair. Amber's artistic touch came alive as she snipped and shaped, adding stylish bangs and layers that accentuated my features. She paused and looked at me through the mirror. "Do you honestly think Jesse might've had something to do with his daddy?"

"Like I said, I don't know yet. I would hope not."

"Same here!"

"Do you know if Jesse is expecting any money from Walter's life insurance policy?"

"Nah. He knows he ain't gonna see that money anytime soon, if ever. There's some stipulations, you see. And he's just too hard-headed."

Ah, yes. The stipulations ... At the moment, Jesse didn't seem too keen on sobering up.

She made a few more little snips, then got out the blow dryer. After she finished styling my hair, she spun me around to face the mirror, her face beaming with pride.

"Alrighty, you're all done. Take a look!"

I examined my reflection, pleasantly surprised by the transformation. The new style softened my features and gave me a more polished look. "Wow, Amber. You really do have a gift."

We walked to the register. "What do I owe you?"

Amber waved her manicured hand dismissively. "This one's on the house."

I was touched by her generosity. "Thank you! You get a month's worth of free Minted Mayhem Lattes!" I gently squeezed her arm. "And thanks for being straightforward about Jesse. I appreciate it."

She handed me her business card with her number on it. "If you find out Jesse was ... you know ... promise you'll be gentle, and let me know, okay? He's a troubled soul, and I'm praying for the best, but I understand if it's the worst."

I nodded, smiling kindly. "I will."

As if on cue, the final notes of Dolly's "Light of a Clear Blue Morning" faded out. The hopeful message felt like an ironic contrast to the murky waters I was wading through.

With my new hairstyle, I left the salon, pondering Amber's words and the question marks surrounding Jesse.

My phone buzzed. Jules's name flashed on the screen, and I answered.

"Parker here."

"Parker," Jules said, her tone crisp and professional. "I'm afraid I need to recalibrate our dinner plans. An unforeseen circumstance has arisen, requiring my immediate attention."

"No problem," I replied.

"Can we reschedule for tomorrow evening?" Jules asked.

"My schedule is wide open."

"Excellent. And to mitigate any inconvenience, why don't you take a guest to dinner there tonight? On my tab, of course."

"Thanks. I might just do that." I hung up.

Looks like my dance card just freed up … Truth be told, I wasn't exactly ready to dive into the world of high-stakes business empires just yet. My cozy coffee shop was buzzing along nicely. And with this yo-yo case I was working on, I needed some quality time with Whit. We'd both been swamped lately, and our get-togethers had been few and far between.

I texted Whit: *Dinner tonight @ Old Courthouse? Jules cancelled but is picking up the tab.*

His response came quickly: *The Old Courthouse Grill? You're on. Dress code lawyer-chic?*

I shot back: *Judge's robes required, but gavel optional … [winking eye emoji]*

The message sent, I smiled, anticipating a relaxing evening with Whit and a chance to re-examine the puzzle that was this case.

As I slipped my phone back into my pocket, the evening ahead seemed full of promise—but you know how that goes …

CHAPTER 11

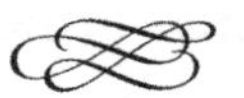

The evening lights of Main Street twinkled around me as I approached The Old Courthouse Grill. It was only three blocks up and over from my cafe, so I told Whit I'd just meet him at the restaurant. My fingers nervously toyed with a stray lock of my newly styled hair. The weight felt different, unfamiliar. I had dressed for a casual winter evening out, wearing a soft cream-colored sweater, fitted black pants and warm boots. Whit rounded the corner, looking effortlessly handsome in a charcoal crew-neck sweater and dark jeans.

He stopped short when he saw me, eyes widening in pleasant surprise.

I smirked, breaking the silence. "What's the matter, Hawthorne? Never seen a woman with bangs before?"

Whit blinked, then a slow smile spread across his face. "Parker Hayes, is that you under all that style?"

"Nope, it's her stylish twin. Much more fashionable, slightly less snarky."

He chuckled, offering his arm. "Well, I must say, stylish-twin-Parker cleans up nicely. I'm having my doubts about the less snarky part, though."

I took his arm, rolling my eyes. "Caught me. And don't get used to it. This whole 'polished' look is more high-maintenance than my coffee grinder."

We turned our attention to the restaurant before us. The Old Courthouse Grill stood imposingly at the end of the street, its stately brick facade and grand columns a testament to its former life as Magnolia Grove's center of justice. Now, instead of handing down verdicts, it doled out overpriced entrees and pretentious wine lists.

"Ready to be judged by the court of culinary snobbery?" I quipped.

Whit grinned. "Lead the way, counselor."

Whit pulled open the heavy oak door, and we stepped into the grand foyer of the restaurant. The transformation from Halls of Justice to Halls of Gastronomy was impressive, to say the least. Crystal chandeliers hung from the vaulted ceilings, casting a luminous glow over the marble floors. The air was thick with the aroma of truffle oil and seared meat.

A hostess, dressed in a crisp black suit that wouldn't have looked out of place on a judge, stood behind a smart wooden podium. She greeted us with a polite smile. "Good evening. Do you have a reservation?"

"Yes, under Winston," I replied, silently thanking Jules.

The hostess nodded, consulting her tablet. "Ah, yes. Please follow me."

She led us through the main dining room, a cavernous

space filled with tables draped in white linen. The walls were adorned with portraits of stern-looking judges and ornate legal documents. I wondered if the ghosts of convicted criminals past were haunting the nooks and crannies.

We arrived at our table, an elegant booth tucked away in a corner. The hostess handed us what looked like leather-bound legal dossiers.

"Your dockets for the evening," she said with a professional but sincere smile. "Your server will be with you shortly."

I flipped open the menu, my eyes widening at the prices. "Good grief, I think I need a lawyer to negotiate these prices."

Whit chuckled, perusing his menu. "I'm pretty sure that pasta dish costs more than my first car."

I scanned the gloriously pretentious descriptions. "What exactly is a 'deconstructed caprese salad with balsamic air'? Did the chef forget how to assemble a salad?"

Whit grinned, leaning in conspiratorially. "I hear it comes with a gavel to smash the tomatoes yourself."

I snorted, hiding my laugh behind the menu. "Order that, and you'll be held in contempt of good taste."

Our banter was interrupted by our server, a polished young man with an affable smile.

"Good evening! My name is Carson, and I will be your server for the evening. May I interest you in our wine selection?"

I shook my head. "Trust me … no one wants me to drink wine."

Whit chuckled, and Carson laughed politely.

"Just water for me, thanks," I said.

"We have artisanal spring water from the mountains or Italian seltzer."

"The spring water sounds perfect," I replied.

Whit nodded in agreement. "Same here."

As Carson departed, I whispered to Whit, "I feel like I should be wearing a powdered wig."

Whit's eyes twinkled. "And muss up your new hairdo?"

I kicked him playfully under the table, blushing.

We settled in to consider our meal options, surrounded by the restaurant's distinguished ambiance. Despite the pretentiousness, the hostess and Carson were genuinely friendly, if a bit formal.

As I deliberated between the "Jury's Choice" ribeye and the "Habeas Corpus" halibut, Jackson Beauregard's smooth voice interrupted the dining room's refined chatter.

"Well, if it isn't Magnolia Grove's newest power couple."

I looked up to find Jackson, impeccably dressed, standing at our table. His tall and waifish date stood beside him, her almond-brown eyes illuminated by the soft light as she took us in.

Whit's tone was cordial yet guarded. "Good evening, Jackson."

I offered a genuine smile. "Fancy meeting you here."

"Barely recognized you. New hairstyle?"

"Mm-hmm."

"Looks nice."

Whit jumped in. "And who's this?"

Jackson puffed up his chest. "Vanessa Graves. I'm

sharing some of our town's hidden gems. Vanessa, these here are Whit Hawthorne, our town historian, and Parker Hayes ... what shall I call you ... cafe owner and freelance murder investigative consultant?"

Vanessa nodded to Whit, then extended her hand toward me, her grip firm. "Nice to meet you, Parker."

"Likewise. What brings you to our little corner of the world, Vanessa?"

"I'm an architect. Jackson's been showing me the revitalization and potential in Magnolia Grove."

"Interesting. Magnolia Grove does seem to be booming."

Jackson gazed at his date with admiration. "Vanessa's as good at what she does as you are at what you do." Jackson turned back to me, his expression serious. "Roger Buzzard mentioned you're investigating Walter Carr's murder."

I had almost forgotten that Jackson Beauregard and Roger Buzzard, Esq. had what I would call a complicated association. Depending on where you landed in their history, you wouldn't be able to tell if they were best friends or mortal enemies.

"Yeah, I'm on the case. Curious to get the Jackson Beauregard take on Lauren Yancey. Guilty or innocent?"

Jackson leaned in, using a low voice. "What would she have to gain? Nothing. One thing I know about her is that she is a very astute businesswoman. I assume you think she's innocent?"

I hesitated, unsure how much to reveal. "Not sure yet."

Jackson frowned. "That doesn't sound like you, Parker. Maybe ask yourself: *cui bono*? It means—"

"I know what it means, Jackson ... who benefits."

Jackson's charming smile returned. "I'm sure Lauren's appreciative to have you helping."

I raised a brow. "Ha! That's one way to put it."

"In other news, I hear Jules Winston is looking to partner up with you."

I pointed at the menu. "She's sponsoring our evening. Giving me the hard sell."

Jackson grinned. "Sounds like her. Some advice: tread wisely. I've done business with her. She can be cut-throat."

"Noted. Thanks, Jackson. Nice meeting you, Vanessa."

With a nod at Whit and me, he guided Vanessa away, leaving me pondering the underlying currents in Magnolia Grove.

I set down my menu. "Jackson Beauregard. Still trying to get a read on that one ..."

Whit fumbled with his napkin. "He's got his finger on the town's pulse, that's for sure."

A thought suddenly struck me. "You know, I've never really delved deeper into the enigma that is Jackson Beauregard. I'm either helping solve his brother's murder or interrogating him for another one. So, tell me, why isn't Magnolia Grove's second most eligible bachelor—you being the first, of course—married?"

Whit's eyes softened, a hint of sadness creeping into his voice. "He was. To Elizabeth. Smartest lady there ever was, next to you, of course. Matter of fact, she sort of was like you: smart, free-spirited, industrious."

"Let me guess, he cheated on her and she left him?" The words tumbled out before I could stop them.

"Parker, you've got to be less cynical about people. She passed on about ten years ago. Huntington's disease. It was rare but aggressive. Jackson immersed himself in his work after she passed on. They had one daughter, Olivia. She finished medical school and now goes to some of the poorest regions on the planet as a missionary doctor."

I felt a lump form in my throat as guilt washed over me. Never would I have imagined such a tragic backstory for the seemingly unflappable Jackson Beauregard. It shed new light on his driven nature and occasional confidence that bordered on arrogance. No wonder I struggled to get a firm read on Jackson—he hid his pain remarkably well.

"I … had no idea," I murmured, feeling a newfound empathy for the man.

Whit reached across the table, giving my hand a gentle squeeze. "There's often more to people than meets the eye, Parker. Even in a small town like ours."

I swallowed hard. Desperate to lighten the mood, I grasped for a change of subject.

"And remind me again, *Whittaker Hawthorne,* why you aren't married?" I forced a playful tone into my voice.

Whit's expression shifted, a Cheshire cat grin spreading across his face. "I'm just waiting for the right person."

His eyes locked with mine, and I felt a flutter in my chest that had nothing to do with guilt or empathy. The air between us seemed to crackle with unspoken possibilities.

Before I could formulate a response, Carson, our waiter, materialized at the table, setting down our waters and breaking the moment. "Are you ready to order?"

I cleared my throat, suddenly very interested in the menu. "Yes, I think we are."

Carson pulled out his tablet with a flourish. "Wonderful. What can I get for you this evening?"

I scanned the menu one last time, settling on something that wouldn't completely feel like I was taking advantage of Jules's generosity. "I'll have the 'Habeas Corpus' halibut, please."

Whit nodded approvingly. "And I'll go with the 'Jury's Choice' ribeye, medium rare."

"Splendid selections. Any appetizers?" Carson tapped our orders into his tablet.

"No, thanks," I answered for us.

"I'll have those out to you shortly," Carson said.

After he left, I turned back to Whit. "Let's play a little game of 'cui bono,'" I suggested. "Who benefits from Walter's death?"

Whit's eyes shone with enthusiasm. "Alright. How about Ronald Sweetwater?"

"Ronald, our local ice cream mogul, *almost* had the deal in place to buy Walter's farm. However, we know Walter was reconsidering. Although Ronald *seemed* confident to us that Walter was going to finalize the sale, perhaps he wasn't. Maybe Walter's doubts forced Ronald to act impulsively. Getting Walter out of the picture could've paved the way for Ronald to locate that Promise to Sell document, sign it and seal his claim to the property."

"Plausible ... Then there's George Baxter," Whit said.

"Mr. 'Drop and Give Me Twenty.' While there's no apparent financial gain and he claimed to harbor no resentment, a lifetime of rivalry with Walter could've fostered a revenge murder. I've seen it."

"It's possible, but in my humble opinion, not probable … I have to mention it, Parker, but what about Jules? Wasn't she interested in acquiring that property?"

"Yes, she was interested in it until Walter pivoted because of her association with Lauren. I'm not sure how killing Walter would benefit her."

Whit considered this. "Then there's Jesse Carr."

I played with my fork. "Jesse, Jesse, Jesse. From what Amber said, Jesse's not willing or able to cash in on the life insurance policy due to some of its more … challenging clauses. So he wouldn't have done it for the life insurance."

Whit added, "But what about the property? If there's no legally binding document that says otherwise, he inherits the farm, doesn't he?"

"Yep. So far, it looks like Jesse would benefit the most. Also, he thoroughly detests Lauren. Framing her for the murder would be the icing on the cake."

Whit sat back against the booth. "Wow. I don't want to believe Jesse is capable of doing something like that, but logically, it makes the most sense."

I shrugged. "Motive, opportunity, and instability—and resentment toward his father—it's a plausible theory."

Whit reached across the table and held my hand. "I know you're eager to solve this, but why don't we take a break and pick this up tomorrow? Tonight, let's relax and enjoy the evening."

Our conversation was interrupted by Carson's return with our meals.

He set the plates before us. "Enjoy your dinner."

The aroma of perfectly seasoned halibut wafted up, and I couldn't wait to take a bite. The pan-seared fish flaked easily, its tender flesh infused with a subtle lemon-dill sauce. Alongside the halibut, steamed asparagus spears retained their crispness, drizzled with a light hollandaise that added richness without overpowering the delicate flavors.

Whit, meanwhile, dug into his grilled ribeye, the sizzle of the sear giving way to a juicy, pink center. His eyes lit up as he took his first bite, the charred crust and savory flavors hitting the spot. He then took a bite of the twice-baked potato alongside his steak. "Mmm, perfect."

The mystery momentarily took a backseat as we savored the exquisite flavors of The Old Courthouse Grill. The warm ambiance, complete with rustic wood accents and soft jazz, enveloped us in a sense of relaxation.

We ate in comfortable silence for a few minutes, the only sound the clinking of silverware and muted conversation from nearby tables.

After we finished our meal, Carson returned to our table. "I see by the empty plates you enjoyed the food?"

I nodded while Whit gave a thumbs-up. "Top notch."

"Would you like to hear our dessert docket?"

Whit and I simultaneously bobbed our heads.

"We've got our famous bourbon pecan pie, chocolate lava cake, or a seasonal berry crumble. Which one strikes your fancy?"

Whit and I exchanged a glance. "We'll share the chocolate lava cake," Whit said.

Carson smiled. "Excellent choice. I'll bring an extra spoon."

He gathered our dishes and walked away.

Whit leaned in, the flecks of gold twinkling in his warm brown eyes. "So, Parker, despite all the happenings, are you happy about moving here?"

I smirked. "I'm getting used to it."

Whit chuckled. "You'll get there, city girl."

Carson returned with the chocolate lava cake, two spoons balanced on the rim of the plate. The warm cake split open at the gentlest touch, releasing a river of dark chocolate that pooled decadently on the pristine white china.

I watched the molten chocolate mix with the rich cake. "Mmm ... Looks like heaven in dessert form." I took a bite and moaned. "Death by chocolate, and what a way to go."

Whit took a heaping spoonful and closed his eyes in bliss. We took turns digging in, savoring the flavors.

When we were finished, Whit sat back, satisfied. "The verdict is in … The Old Courthouse Grill has won my heart."

I scraped the last of the chocolate syrup from the plate. "Guilty as charged. Best culinary renovation in town."

"The defense rests. Case closed."

Warmth spread through my chest. Spending time with Whit never fell short.

We finished up, thanking Carson for the marvelous meal and service, and then we strolled out of the restored courthouse.

Whit took my hand as we walked. "So, we had the

verdict on the restaurant. What's the verdict on the evening?"

I rested my head against his shoulder. "It's unanimous: tonight was a victory."

Whit's eyes sparkled. "I concur. We'll have to thank Jules for sponsoring it."

We reached the backdoor of the cafe and stood under the glow of the light.

"Thanks for coming out to dinner, Whit."

His gaze locked onto mine. "My pleasure, Parker."

He leaned in, his lips pressing against mine in a soft, gentle kiss we held for a few moments while the world around us slipped away.

As Whit's lips left mine, the night air seemed to vibrate with possibility.

"Goodnight, counselor," he whispered, his eyes crinkling at the corners.

The world narrowed to the space between us, the mystery and mayhem temporarily forgotten. For a moment, I was just a girl standing in front of a boy, feeling the sparks of something wonderful. But as quickly as the moment came, reality rushed back in. We had a case to solve, a killer to catch.

CHAPTER 12

My day began with Major greeting me with a thorough face-licking as he wriggled around the covers.

"Alright, alright," I mumbled, gently pushing his furry face away. "I'm up. No need to drown me in doggy drool."

Sunlight streamed through the curtains, painting my apartment above Catch You Latte in a golden glow. The aroma of brewing coffee and Hazel's snickerdoodles wafted up from the cafe below, a tantalizing promise of the day ahead.

I stretched, reveling in the rare feeling of being well-rested. For once, my dreams hadn't been plagued by visions of murder weapons or mysterious cheese-related clues. A good night's sleep had done wonders for my outlook.

"Today's the day, Major," I said, scratching behind his ears. "We're going to crack this case wide open. I can feel it in my bones."

Major tilted his head, his expression a mix of canine confusion and unbridled enthusiasm.

"Don't give me that look," I chuckled. "Your investigative skills are second to none. Who else can sniff out a hidden treat in record time?"

My furry partner wagged his tail in agreement.

I swung my legs over the side of the bed, my bare feet touching the cool hardwood floor. The contrast sent a shiver through my body, jolting me fully awake. My mind began to charge, piecing together the puzzle of Walter Carr's murder.

Lauren Yancey, the artisanal cheese maven, was still the prime suspect in the eyes of the law. But my gut told me there was more to this story. Jesse Carr, Walter's troubled son, had seemed to leave his trademark scent—beer—at Lauren's apartment, along with some potato chip crumbs, suggesting he was the one who planted evidence to incriminate her.

Major jumped off the bed and trotted beside me as I walked down the hall to the kitchenette. "What do you think, Major? Should we start with a strong cup of coffee or dive right into detective work?"

Major stood next to his food bowl, looking at me expectantly.

"Right." I laughed. "Breakfast first. Then we save the day."

After feeding Major and going through my morning routine, we both headed downstairs. The delicious scent of cookies baking grew stronger with each step. The kitchen was already its usual disaster zone, so that meant Hazel was already full-steam ahead. I exited the kitchen and entered the cafe proper, where Hazel was bustling around, her mint-colored hair bobbing as she wiped down the tables.

"Morning, boss! Morning, Major!" she chirped.

"Morning, Hazel. Everything ship-shape?"

"Aye aye, captain!" She saluted with a dish towel.

I chuckled, flipping the "CLOSED" sign to "OPEN" and heading back to the counter.

Hazel handed me a steaming mug of Ethiopian Yirgacheffe, its bright citrus and floral notes mingling with subtle hints of bergamot and dark chocolate. I inhaled deeply, savoring the rich scent before taking a sip. The caffeine hit my system, sharpening my focus for the day ahead.

I texted Whit: *Morning, sunshine. How's your day looking?*

His reply came quickly: *Bright and beautiful, like your smile. Can't stop thinking about last night.*

I rolled my eyes, grinning despite myself and texted: *Sappy, but sweet! What's on your agenda?*

He texted: *More tunnel discussions with Rufus. You?*

Going to interview Jesse again ...

Please be careful, Parker.

You know me! [winking emoji]

I took out Amber's card and dialed her number.

She picked up on the second ring. "Amber's Hair Affairs."

"Hey, it's Parker Hayes."

"Parker! What a nice surprise. How's that new 'do treating you?"

"It's great, Amber. Thanks again. Listen, I was hoping to talk to Jesse, but I don't want to drop by unannounced, and I realized I don't have his number."

A pause hung in the air. "I can give you his number, but he ain't around. Went on a business trip."

My eyebrows shot up. "A business trip?"

Amber's tone was laced with annoyance and amusement. "Yeah, I know, right? That turkey was supposed to pick me up after work yesterday, but he didn't show. I called everywhere. Rowan from Double Barrel Roadhouse said he was there yesterday morning, and Taylor—that's my brother—said he saw him at Lucky Lou's earlier in the day as well. But after that, nobody saw him. Tricia—that's my sister—had to give me a lift home. Then he texts me last night, 'Sorry, darlin', sudden business trip.' Business trip, my eye."

I found myself chuckling at Amber's sarcasm. "Is this usual?"

Amber laughed. "No. My guess is he's on a bender."

"Right. Well, can you text me his number? I'd like to try to get a hold of him about the case."

"Sure thing. Take care."

Amber hung up, then sent the number, and I quickly shot Jesse a text: *Jesse, Parker here. Hope you're doing well. Just want to follow up on a few things. Thanks.*

I pocketed my phone, tucked my notebook into my bag and slipped on my coat. "Hey, Hazel. You did a great job yesterday with the morning rush. You up for it again?"

"You know it!"

"Great. I'll be back before lunch. Thanks, Hazel."

Major, my loyal companion and I stepped out into the crisp morning air. The chilly breeze cut through the town of Magnolia Grove, infusing me with energy and determination. I felt invigorated, ready to unravel the tangled threads of Walter Carr's murder.

"Time to retrace Jesse's steps," I said to Major, who gave an animated bark.

Our first stop after picking up Bertha—Clyde's trusty old Buick Roadmaster station wagon—would be the Double Barrel Roadhouse.

As we walked the ten minutes to Clyde's, the town's quaint charm almost made me forget the darkness of the case. I wondered if Jesse's vanishing act was more than just a bender, if perhaps it was connected to Walter's murder.

Bertha waited for us in Clyde's driveway, her worn chrome gleaming in the afternoon sun. I loaded Major in.

"Alright, old girl," I said, turning the key.

Bertha's engine coughed, sputtered, and finally roared to life. The defrost kicked in, blowing warm air that carried the scent of worn leather and aged wood.

The FM radio crackled on, tuning in to Clyde's favorite station: WHAY 103.5, playing the best of classic country and bluegrass. Hank Williams Sr.'s "Hey, Good Lookin'" filled the car, and I chuckled.

We set off, leaving the charming neighborhood behind. I guided Bertha out of inner Magnolia Grove, heading eastward toward the outskirts of town. The quaint houses gave way to more utilitarian buildings, and the winding back road spat us out in front of a weathered wooden structure that seemed to have been plucked straight from a biker movie.

The sprawling dirt lot, home to a lone pickup truck, stretched out before us like a barren welcome mat. A faded marquee creaked in the gentle breeze, boasting:

"Double Barrel Roadhouse: Where the Good Times Roll & the Whiskey Flows" in crooked, hand-painted letters. A rough-around-the-edges sign below added:

"'Moonshine Mavericks' Live Music Fri & Sat | Bike Night Tues | Pool Tables & Cold Beer"

Bertha's tires crunched on the gravel as we pulled into the lot.

I raised an eyebrow. "Not exactly the Ritz, eh, Major?"

I parked, shifted the column shifter into park, killed the engine and climbed out, Major trotting faithfully beside me. The "CLOSED" sign on the door didn't deter me; I rapped my knuckles against the weathered wood, hoping for a bit of luck.

After a brief pause, the creaky door swung open, revealing a woman with a tough-as-nails aura. Her silver hair was pulled back into a ponytail that screamed, "don't mess with me." Despite the early hour, her eyes sparkled with a sharp, been-around-the-block alertness. A pen perched behind her ear and reading glasses hung around her neck, hinting at interrupted paperwork. She gave me the once-over, her gaze lingering on my hair and then boots.

"We don't open until eleven," she drawled, her voice seasoned with the grit of someone who'd seen (and possibly instigated) their fair share of rowdy nights.

I flashed my most disarming smile. "Just a few questions, please? It's about a missing person."

Her gaze held on me for a beat, her eyes narrowing slightly as if sizing me up before drifting down to Major, where a hint of a smirk appeared. "Cute dog." With a nod, she stepped aside, beckoning us into the Roadhouse's depths with a sweep of her arm. "Ask your questions but make 'em quick. I've got books to cook ... I mean, balance." She winked, the corner of her mouth twitching upward, hinting at a mischievous manner.

As we entered, the interior of the Double Barrel enveloped us in its worn but down-home atmosphere—all dark wood accents, neon beer signs casting a colorful glow and the scent of citrus-based disinfectant struggling to overpower the lingering aromas of stale beer and whiskey. A sign above the bar caught my eye:

"NO SMOKING INSIDE (We Mean It. Seriously) Light up in here, and you'll be: 1. Kicked out (no refunds) 2. Banned for life (don't test us) 3. Have to deal with our bartender Ree (trust us, she's tougher than she looks)"

A jukebox stood silent in the corner, its metal skin adorned with stickers and scratches, waiting for the day's first quarter to bring it to life. Off in a corner area were two pool tables, a dartboard and a shuffleboard table.

"I'm Rowan, by the way. Call me Ro." Her husky drawl smoothed out the edges like fine-grit sandpaper.

"I'm Parker," I replied, nodding in appreciation. "This is Major."

My sidekick scanned the surroundings with a happy-go-lucky eye.

Ro gave a curt half-smile. "Can I offer you anything? Beer, seltzer, or maybe some peanuts?"

"I think I'm good for now, Ro. Thanks." Yesterday's "Magnolia Maniac diet" was officially over.

Ro led me to a cozy booth, where a scattering of paperwork and ledgers awaited her attention. I slid into the worn, cushioned seat, Major settling comfortably at my feet beneath the table. Ro sat across from me, her movements economical as she picked up her pen, slipped on her reading glasses and began to multitask with ease.

"You mentioned a missing person," she said, her eyes scanning the documents in front of her.

"Yeah, Jesse Carr. He was here yesterday. I'm trying to piece together his movements."

Ro's pen paused mid-scratch. She looked up, her eyes sharp over the rim of her glasses. "Jesse Carr, huh? Walter's boy."

I nodded, leaning in slightly. "That's the one. Did you see him?"

Ro set her pen down, giving me her full attention. "Oh, I saw him alright. Hard to miss. He came in right about this time."

"Did you notice anything noteworthy?"

"Noteworthy? Sure. First off, I ain't ever seen him before noon. Then he starts flashin' money in my face like it was burnin' a hole in his pocket. Talkin' about his debts being cleared and things finally lookin' up. Says he's gonna be real flush soon and askin' me if I'd like to partner up with him on opening up a little beer spot in town. Braggin' how he's got connections."

I jotted this down in my notebook. I pieced together the timeline: after Whit and I saw him at his trailer yesterday morning, he dropped off Amber at the salon then came here.

"Did he mention anything specific about these debts or his sudden windfall?"

Ro's brow furrowed in thought. "Not really."

"Anything else stand out?"

"Sure. A young lady comes in, and they go over to that booth right over there and have a chat."

"Young lady? Do you know who?"

"Never seen her before. Smart-lookin' gal, petite with dark hair pulled back neat and tidy. Professional type. Maybe thirty."

"Any idea what they talked about?"

"Naw. At first, looked like business. Then she got earnest, though, like she was trying to console him. Took his hand and such. Then she left. Whole deal lasted maybe five minutes." Ro set down her pen and leaned back, crossing her arms. "He got a bit tearful after that. Started apologizing out loud to his deceased daddy over and over. It was a bit awkward."

I raised an eyebrow. "Then what?"

"Then he yelled something about sellin' out to city slickers, the cheese lady going down and how justice was finally gonna be served. I reckoned he was venting about that lady charged with his daddy's murder. Got up, marched right out without as much as a goodbye, slammin' the door behind him, knocking the dang neon Lucky's Lager sign askew. He peeled out of the parking lot in that brand-new truck of his, nearly taking out Rooster's motorcycle."

"He left by himself?"

"Yup. So he's gone missing, huh?"

"According to Amber, he went on a 'business trip.' You wouldn't have any ideas about that?"

Ro picked up her pen and tapped it on the table. "Nah. That kid's all over the map. Always has bright ideas and cookin' up something, but he's always been all hat and no cattle. Guess maybe he's got some traction with somethin' this time around. What that something is, I have no idea. Course, he might just be on a bender."

I tucked a few strands of hair behind my ear, processing this information. "Thanks, Ro. You've been incredibly helpful."

As I stood to leave, Ro's voice stopped me. "Hey, Parker? If you run into him, tell him he still owes me an apology. And ... make sure he's okay, will you? Kid's gotten a few bad hands and made some wrong turns but ..."

I met her gaze, noting the concern behind her tough exterior. "I'll do my best, Ro. Thanks again."

Major and I stepped back into the crisp morning air, and my mind was in overdrive. Jesse's behavior at the Double Barrel Roadhouse had painted a disturbing picture. The pieces were starting to fall into place, but I had a gut feeling that I was missing a few crucial ones—like the identity of the mysterious young woman and whatever she said that had possibly set Jesse off.

The drive to Lucky Lou's Pawn Shop took us to another part of the outer reaches of town, where industrial buildings and warehouses dotted the landscape like scattered building blocks. We passed by a rusted water tower, its once-vibrant logo now faded to a ghostly silhouette. The road narrowed, and the pavement gave way to a patchwork of asphalt and gravel.

Lou's shop occupied a weathered brick structure that had seen better days, its faded sign barely legible in the winter light. The neon sign above the door still had missing letters and read: *ucky Lou's Paw and Lo n.* Guess old Lou hadn't gotten around to fixing it yet.

The dirt parking lot, cut in half by an old railroad track, was empty except for a beautifully restored Ford Bronco. Weeds pushed through the cracks in the pavement, resilient in the face of neglect.

As we entered, the bell above the door jingled, its bright tone a contrast to the shop's worn exterior. The interior was a treasure trove of eclectic clutter: rows of dusty shelves overflowing with tools, electronics and mysterious contraptions. Glass cases showcased jewelry, coins and firearms, each item tagged with a handwritten price.

Lou squinted at us from behind the counter, his stocky frame hunched over a display case. His receding hairline and the gleam of multiple rings on his fingers caught the shop's fluorescent light. "If it ain't my favorite crime solver. Barely recognized you with that hairstyle. Looks good. Been a while, Hayes."

"Hi there, Lou. Yeah, haven't seen you since the Beauregard case," I replied, recalling our last encounter. I leaned against the glass counter, careful not to smudge it with my fingerprints. Lou was particular about his displays.

Lou's gaze shifted to Major, who was sniffing curiously at a nearby shelf of old radios. "Who's your new partner in crime?"

"This is Major," I said, giving the leash a gentle tug to bring him closer.

"I'll be right back," Lou grunted, his joints creaking as he pushed himself away from the counter. He disappeared into the back room, the beaded curtain clinking behind him. He returned moments later, rounding the counter with surprising agility for a man his size.

"Can you sit, Major?" Lou asked, his gruff voice softening slightly. Major promptly sat, tail thumping against the linoleum floor.

Lou opened his palm, revealing a small bone chew treat. He gave it to Major, his ringed fingers scratching under the dog's chin. "There's a good boy." Major immediately began gnawing on the bone obsessively, the sound echoing in the cluttered shop.

Lou straightened up, his eyes almost hidden beneath his bushy eyebrows. "What can I do ya for?"

"Jesse Carr." I cut straight to the chase.

Lou loudly exhaled from his nose, a sound somewhere between a snort and a sigh. He walked back around the counter, his hands automatically reaching for a rag to wipe the already gleaming glass. "If that fella ever got off the sauce, he'd be head of a company ... but ain't that like life ... bunch of *only ifs*." He looked up at me, his eyes sharp despite his world-weary tone. "What you wanna know?"

"What time was he here yesterday?"

Lou continued his methodical cleaning, though his eyes

never left mine. "Just before noon, which sort of shocked me. Never seen him that early before." He paused, his brow furrowing. "You thinkin' he had something to do with his daddy's deal?"

My mind went into analysis mode. This would've meant Jesse came here after he left the Double Barrel. I kept my face neutral. "I don't know if he had anything to do with it. I'm trying to piece this together. Why was he here?"

"Get his stuff outta hock. Sorta took me aback. He was flush with cash."

"Anything else?"

"Sure. Said he was gonna go shootin' in the hills, so he bought a box of rounds, which I thought was a bit peculiar."

"Peculiar? Why?"

Lou leaned in, his voice dropping as if sharing a secret. "As far as I know, I've sold him the only three guns he owns. Those being a Remington 870 12-gauge shotgun, a Ruger 10/22 .22 caliber rifle and a Smith & Wesson Model 642 .38 special revolver. But the box of rounds he bought were for a 9mm."

Goosebumps rose on my neck. The exact caliber of the one used to kill Walter.

"Anything else?" I tried to keep my voice steady.

"I had to ask him to park his beer outside. Walked in with an open can like it was a soda pop. Par for the course for him, though. That man likes his suds." He shook his head, amusement and resignation on his face.

"Thanks, Lou. You've been very helpful."

"The pleasure was mine. Don't be such a stranger. Adios, Major."

Major ignored him, too busy with the bone.

As I walked toward the exit, something caught my eye. I stopped in front of a small vending machine with snacks near the door.

"Did he happen to buy anything out of this machine?"

Lou's bushy eyebrows shot up. "Now that you mention it, he did. Bought a candy bar … and a bag of chips."

I nodded, my mind already tying together the implications. "Thanks again, Lou. I'll see you around."

Major and I stepped back into the crisp winter air. One thing was clear: the evidence pointed to Jesse. The sticky beer spill and chip fragments on Lauren's floor matched Lou's revelation. And that box of 9mm rounds in her planter? Jesse must have put them there. The timeline was forming … Jesse had left here and gone to Lauren's. After that, he disappeared.

"Come on, Major," I said, heading back to Bertha. "We've got a deputy to talk to."

CHAPTER 13

One of the things about living in Magnolia Grove was that there were plenty of different routes to get to where you needed to go. I opted to take a different way back to town from the one I had traveled. The GPS on my phone began spitting its directions. Major dozed in the passenger seat, his prized bone that Lucky Lou had graciously gifted him still clutched in his jaws.

I gaped in disbelief at the landscape unfolding beyond the windshield. The rural woods and scattered farms I remembered from just six months ago when I'd first moved here had vanished, replaced by bulldozed fields and lots. Bright billboards heralded the arrival of new developments: "Oakwood Estates—Coming Soon!" and "Magnolia Meadows—Luxury Living."

The GPS continued to dole out directions, oblivious to the transformation. Major stirred and sat up, his bone still clutched in his jaws.

I felt like a stranger in my own town. The charm of Magnolia Grove's rural surroundings was rapidly giving way to suburban sprawl. The thought sent a pang of disappointment through me. What had drawn me to this place was its quiet, small-town feel.

"Well, I'll be darned," I muttered, causing Major's ears to perk up. "Looks like progress is marching on whether we like it or not."

I slowed Bertha to a crawl, taking in the transformation. Where old oak trees once stood, now rows of wooden house-frames sprouted from newly bulldozed earth. The air was filled with the cacophony of hammers banging and beeping construction vehicles, drowning out the chirping of birds.

Jackson's question from last night echoed in my mind: Cui bono? Who benefits? Walter's note on the tentative contract with Ronald: NO HOUSING DEVELOPMENTS! The rapid development sprawling before me raised a new suspicion: Perhaps I needed to add "shady developers" to my list of potential suspects.

I patted Major's head, earning a sleepy thump of his tail. "What do you think, buddy? Should we add 'land-hungry opportunists' to our suspect board?"

Major yawned in response, clearly more interested in his bone than the realities of urban sprawl.

While Jesse was still my number-one suspect, perhaps there was a developer angle that tied into the story ... I mulled over the moving parts, and my inner conspiracy theorist took over. Walter's farm would've been prime property for developers looking to cash in on this real-estate boom. Walter's refusal to sell specifically to developers suddenly took on a whole new significance. Perhaps he'd turned down other interested buyers besides Ronald Sweetwater and Jules Winston, and they didn't take too kindly to that. Maybe a greedy developer figured Jesse would be easier to deal with, so they incentivized Jesse's rebellion against his father, resulting in murder. After all, where did Jesse's sudden windfall originate? As the old adage goes, follow the money …

I steered Bertha along the country roads, meandering my way back to town. "Major, let's have a little chat with Deputy Colton. Something tells me this case just got a whole lot bigger than a vat of cheese."

Major's only response was a contented sigh, his bone still firmly lodged in his mouth.

"Yeah, you're right," I said, interpreting his silence as sage wisdom. "Let's hope Colton's more interested in solving this case than these developers are in paving paradise."

THE SHERIFF'S station loomed ahead, its standalone brick façade standing out among the quieter storefronts just outside the old town proper. I pulled Bertha into a spot, her ancient suspension groaning in relief.

"Come on, Scooby Clue," I said, clipping Major's leash to his collar. "Time to dazzle the law enforcement with your investigative prowess." He picked up his bone and jumped out of the car.

We entered the station, the familiar scent of stale coffee and bureaucracy assaulting my nostrils. Leigh Ann sat behind the front desk, her fingers flying over her phone screen with superhuman speed. She didn't even glance up as we approached. Nothing new there.

I fixed on my friendliest smile. "Morning, Leigh Ann. Is Deputy Colton in?"

Her eyes remained glued to her phone. "Mmhmm."

I fought the urge to roll my eyes. "Great. Mind if we wait here?"

She shrugged, still not looking up.

Major, apparently fed up with being ignored, let out a small whine. Leigh Ann's head snapped up so fast I thought she might get whiplash.

"Oh. My. Gosh!" she squealed, her eyes lighting up. "Who is this cutie pie?"

"This is Major," I said, unable to keep the amusement out of my voice. "Clyde Honeycutt's dog. I'm dog-sitting."

Leigh Ann was already out from behind the front desk, cooing and fussing over Major like he was a celebrity. Major, the little ham, ate up the attention, his tail wagging so hard his whole body shook.

Leigh Ann gushed, snapping photos with her phone. "He's so photogenic! And adorable with that bone! Can I post on my Insta?"

"Knock yourself out." I laughed as she attempted to arrange Major into various poses. This was the most enthusiasm I'd ever seen Leigh Ann give to anything besides scrolling.

Mental note: Major was now my official sheriff's station liaison—his charm was unstoppable.

"Work it, handsome! Give me blue steel!" Leigh Ann directed, snapping away.

Major, bless his heart, seemed to understand. He tilted his head, giving the camera a soulful look that would put any influencer to shame.

"Parker?" Deputy Colton's voice broke through the impromptu photoshoot. He stood in the doorway to the back offices, his eyebrows raised in a mix of confusion and amusement.

"Hey, Colton," I said, gently tugging Major away from his admirer. "Can I grab a minute?"

Colton's expression turned serious. "The Walter Carr case, I presume?" He shook his head.

"I've got new evidence. Will you hear me out?"

Colton inhaled deeply, then exhaled through his nostrils with a force that made his magnificent mustache ripple. "Alright, let's talk." He gestured for me to follow him.

We walked to a bustling area filled with desks where several deputies worked. Colton sat down at his, surrounded by familiar clutter. A framed photo caught my eye: generations of his family gathered around him and his wife, beaming with pride.

Colton sat up straight and businesslike. "The hair sample results should be back anytime. Sheriff Sinclair returns tomorrow. She's pushing to close the Carr case quickly."

I felt a knot form in my stomach. Time was running out, and I still had more questions than answers.

"So, what do you got?" Colton rubbed his pushbroom mustache.

Major flopped down at my feet, clearly tuckered out from his modeling session but not tuckered enough to neglect guarding his bone. I took a deep breath, ready to lay out my theories and hoping against hope that Colton would listen. I leaned forward, my elbows on his cluttered desk. "I've got reason to believe Jesse Carr might be involved in his father's murder."

A faint crease formed between Colton's eyebrows, a subtle sign of frustration. "Thought we'd put that to bed, Parker. What've you uncovered now?"

I laid out my evidence, painting a picture of Jesse's suspicious behavior: his sudden influx of cash, his ramblings at the Double Barrel, and the 9mm ammo purchase.

"And get this," I said, my enthusiasm growing. "I found potato chip crumbs and a beer spill at Lauren's place—the same snack and beverage Jesse was seen with at Lucky Lou's Pawn Shop earlier that day. I'm presuming he left the pawn shop, went to Lauren's, planted the evidence, and then you guys showed up and found it." My eyes locked onto Colton's. "By the way, now that I think about it, why did you suddenly choose yesterday afternoon to search Lauren's apartment? Did someone anonymously tip you off, perchance?"

Colton's expression flickered with surprise before settling into a mask of neutrality. He leaned back, steepling his fingers. "Parker, I can't share our procedure with you." His tone was measured, but a hint of skepticism crept in. "Let's focus on your evidence. 9mm rounds—one of the most common calibers—and some potato chip crumbs and beer spillage ... That's what you're hanging your hat on?"

My cheeks flushed. "It's more than that. The sudden cashflow ... the developers sharking around ... the timeline—"

"Now, Parker." Colton cut me off, his tone sincere but firm. "I know you're like a bloodhound and twice as smart, but how do you know Lauren didn't plant that beer spill and potato chips to throw you off her scent, knowing you'd go on and suspect Jesse?"

I opened my mouth to argue, but he pressed on.

"Plus, there was no forced entry. Does Jesse seem like the stealthy lock-pick type? Especially if he's spillin' beer everywhere?"

"But—"

"Or did Lauren give him a spare key, just in case?"

"But—"

"Or did she keep it under the mat, and he just got lucky and found it? Listen up: I've got hard evidence," Colton said, tapping a file on his desk. "You've got nothing but circumstantial crumbs. Literally."

I clenched my jaw, frustration bubbling up inside me. "What about Lauren's alibi?"

"Oh, come now, Parker—she coulda let Bessie out earlier that day. And as far as that cockamamie statue tip?

She coulda done that right before or after she shot him. Fact is, we tracked her cell phone data, and it tells us one thing: it was on the festival grounds the entire time. Period. End of story." Colton lightly slapped the desk to punctuate his point. Then his expression softened slightly. "Look, I appreciate your … enthusiasm. But Sheriff'll be back tomorrow, and that'll be that. Lauren Yancey's goin' behind bars for this."

I stood up, my chair scraping against the linoleum. "I strongly feel you're making a mistake, Deputy Colton."

He shrugged. "Maybe so. But it's not my mistake to make. Sheriff calls the shots, and she's 100% signed off on it."

I nodded curtly, exasperation simmering beneath the surface. "Alright. Thanks for your time."

As I turned to leave, Colton's voice stopped me.

"Parker?"

I turned back, my eyes meeting his. "Yes, Deputy?"

A hint of a smile formed on his lips. "I like the new hair-do. Suits you."

Despite my angst, a smile crept onto my face. "Thanks."

I trudged out of the sheriff's office, Major faithfully trotting by my side. The weight of defeat settled in like a fog clinging to the hills. Maybe it was time to throw in the towel. Even if Lauren was innocent, it seemed like the deck was stacked against her.

We stepped into the crisp afternoon air, the chill slapping my face. Major sensed my mood and nuzzled my leg. I scratched his ears, finding solace in his silent companionship. I yanked open Bertha's creaky door, my discouragement leaking out like the oil from the old station wagon. Major hopped in, still clutching his prized bone, blissfully unaware of our setback.

"Well, that was about as useful as a screen door on a submarine," I grumbled, jamming the key into the ignition.

The sudden chirp of my phone cut through my brooding. I fished it out of my pocket, surprised to see Jules Winston's name on the screen.

"Hi there, Jules."

"Parker," Jules's smooth voice greeted me. "How are you?"

"Best as I can be."

"I trust you enjoyed The Old Courthouse Grill last night?"

I smirked, grateful to set my mind on something other than the stalled-out case. "Oh, it was a regular gastronomic delight. I particularly enjoyed the 'Habeas Corpus' halibut, though I think it cost more than my building."

Jules chuckled softly. "I'm glad you enjoyed it. Listen, about dinner tonight—I was wondering if we could pivot and make it an afternoon with sandwiches instead? I want to show you something."

"Sure. When and where?"

"How about 3 PM? The Whistle Stop."

I glanced at my phone; it was just past eleven. "Alright, Jules. I'll see you at three."

After hanging up, I guided Bertha on the short drive back to Catch You Latte. With a few hours to spare, I had a lunch rush to help Hazel with and a decision to make on how to proceed with Lauren's case. I pulled into a spot behind the cafe and parked.

"Come on, Major. Let's see if Hazel has any of those doggy treats left for you." Major gave me a sideways glance, ensuring I wouldn't take his prized bone.

"Don't worry, buddy. That's yours," I reassured him.

He wagged his tail, bone still firmly in his mouth, and jumped out of the car.

As we entered through the back door, that warm, nutty fragrance of just-brewed coffee curled around me, and the inviting scent of chocolate chip cookies filled the air. For a moment, I forgot about murdered dairy farmers, evidence planters and real-estate developers.

At the counter, Hazel greeted us with a wave. "Hey, Parker! Hey, Major! Guess what I have for you, little guy!" She pulled a dog treat from one of the coffee tins I stored them in and offered it to Major.

He hesitated, unsure what to do with the bone still clutched in his jaws. He cautiously set it down at his paws, eyeing it protectively, before accepting the treat from Hazel.

THE LUNCH RUSH hit Catch You Latte like a caffeine-fueled tornado. We worked in perfect flow in a seamless symphony of coffee pours and pastry exchanges.

As the crowd thinned, I snuck a glance at my phone. Still no text back from Jesse, though he'd read my message. A little before three o'clock, I took off my apron.

"Hazel, I gotta meet with Jules; you good to hold down the fort?" I grabbed my coat.

"Really?! You're going to do business with her?"

"Slow your roll. We're just talking …"

"Okay, boss," she chirped, giving me a thumbs-up.

I left Major snoozing in my apartment, his cherished bone cradled in his paws, and climbed into Bertha. Heading east, I passed through the eclectic Fusion District, where historic homes and worn warehouses stood alongside trendy lofts and local shops. The once-neglected area was slowly transforming, its industrial roots still visible beneath the veneer of gentrification.

I pulled Bertha into a parking spot in the adjacent Switchyard District, where abandoned factories had been reborn as a vibrant open-air mall. A few trendy boutiques and eateries now thrived alongside the old railroad tracks.

Jules waved from the entrance of the Whistle Stop, a sandwich shop nestled within a restored historic locomotive shed, its weathered metal now gleaming with new life.

Inside, the atmosphere was relaxed, caught between the lunch rush and dinner bustle. Yet, the air remained electric, permeated with the scent of baked bread and simmering soups. Exposed brick walls, industrial metal beams and Edison bulbs created a stylishly rustic ambiance.

We joined the short queue at the counter, where two bright-eyed servers, aprons sporting the Whistle Stop's logo—a stylized railroad sign with a sandwich replacing the railroad tracks, accompanied by the phrase, "Whistle Stop Sandwiches: All Aboard for Flavor"—greeted us with welcoming smiles. The occasional hiss of steaming milk, clinking glasses and muffled chatter filled the space with an inviting feel.

Jules gestured to the kitchen. "Everything here is locally sourced and organic. The menu changes with the seasons."

I nodded, impressed. The chalkboard menu boasted sandwiches with names like "The Conductor's Special" and "The Caboose Crusher."

At the counter, Jules ordered the "Smokestack Club" with sweet potato fries and mixed greens, while I opted for the "Turkey Tunnel Vision"—oven-roasted turkey, crisp lettuce, tomato and avocado on a toasted baguette paired with a side of creamy tomato soup.

As we waited for our order, Jules turned to me, her eyes shining.

"So, Parker, what do you think—locally owned or not?"

I surveyed the Whistle Stop's interior, taking in the vintage railroad signs, reclaimed wood accents and eclectic industrial decor. The staff moved with a genuine enthusiasm that added to the charm.

"Feels local."

Jules's lips curved into a sly smile. "What if I told you it wasn't?"

Our order number was called, and we collected our sandwiches. Jules led us to a table by the window, overlooking the Switchyard District's central plaza. The winter landscape outside was serene: bare trees, an empty fountain and benches all bathed in the pale January light.

I unwrapped my turkey sandwich and took a bite. The crunch of crisp lettuce, the tenderness of oven-roasted turkey and the subtle tang of creamy avocado melded together in perfect harmony. A hint of smoky bacon and a drizzle of herb-infused mayo added depth to each bite. "Mmm. This is good … So, this place isn't local? I'm intrigued."

Jules savored a bite of her Smokestack Club, her eyes sparkling with exuberance. "It started as a single shop in a small town outside Charlotte. Now, Whistle Stop has seven locations in North Carolina, with an eighth on the way. Plus two in South Carolina and one in Tennessee."

I froze, sandwich midway to my mouth, stunned. "Seriously? How long did that take?"

Jules's voice dropped to a conspiratorial whisper. "Five years. From one humble shop to ten. And last year's revenue? 12.3 million."

I set my turkey sandwich down, my mind reeling. "That's … astonishing. Quite a leap from a mom-and-pop operation."

Jules nodded, clearly pleased with my reaction. "Streamlined business model, and my PR team is top notch. And that's what I envision for Catch You Latte, Parker. Strategic growth, retaining its charm, character, heart and soul. Imagine sharing that unique experience with more people. You'd be giving them a delightful opportunity to connect with something special."

Her words were persuasive, almost making me feel like not expanding would be a disservice to the world. As we continued our meal, I felt both excitement and trepidation. The potential was thrilling, but was I ready for that kind of expansion?

Jules finished her sandwich and dabbed the side of her

mouth with a napkin. She leaned in, her voice gentle but urgent. "No pressure, Parker. But the sooner we move, the better. Once this Lauren fiasco is figured out, I'll be heading back to Charlotte to meet with investors. I'd love to present them with a solid Catch You Latte plan."

I nodded noncommittally. "I'll consider it. I'll get back to you soon." I lifted my spoon to my lips, savoring the warmth of the creamy tomato soup. The rich broth coated my tongue, infused with subtle hints of basil and a touch of smoky paprika. A dollop of heavy cream added depth, balancing out the tanginess of fresh tomatoes.

Jules's eyes locked onto mine with an inquisitive gaze "Speaking of Lauren, she mentioned someone broke into her apartment and planted evidence?"

I set my spoon down, the warmth and flavor of the soup lingering "Yeah, it was sloppy amateur hour. Whoever did it left a trail of potato chip crumbs and a beer stain."

Jules's brow furrowed. "Any idea who it could've been?"

I hesitated, my tone firm. "I'd rather not disclose that."

Jules nodded graciously. "Of course. Client confidentiality and all that. Is it enough to get Lauren off?"

I sighed, the weight of the investigation settling in. "So far, nope. The evidence is still circumstantial."

Jules's voice was tinged with disappointment. "That's a shame. I'm sure you're doing all you can, Parker. But one thing I've learned in business: if it's a losing proposition, cut your losses."

"What are you saying?"

"I'm saying—and I hate thinking this—that maybe Lauren isn't innocent."

"Do you know something I don't, Jules?"

Jules opened her mouth to respond, but her phone buzzed. She glanced at the screen, her face tightening almost imperceptibly. "I'm so sorry to do this, Parker. I have to run." She stood up abruptly, gathering her things. "Think about my offer, will you? And don't work too hard on this case. Sometimes these things have a way of … resolving themselves."

As Jules rushed out of the sandwich shop, phone pressed to her ear, I caught her murmuring, "Launch it," before the door swung shut. I retrieved my phone and navigated to Whit's number, my thumb hesitating over the call button as a familiar thread of paranoia began to weave through my mind.

What if Jules's interest in expanding my business wasn't just about coffee? Could Jules be using her interest in my business as a diversionary tactic?

The haunting Unsolved Mysteries theme song echoed through the sandwich shop as my phone vibrated in my pocket. I pulled it out and grinned at the contact photo—Hazel giving an enthusiastic thumbs-up, covered head to toe in flour, standing proudly in front of what looked like a flour bomb explosion in my kitchen. She'd insisted on the ringtone, claiming, "because we're, like, actual mystery solvers now!"

"Hey," I answered.

"Parker, we've got a problem." Her voice was laced with urgency.

"What's going on? Please don't tell me you burned down the kitchen …"

"No. Our social media is blowing up, but not in a good way."

"Just give me the gist."

"It's getting ugly. People are claiming we're in cahoots with a 'cow-abusing, statue-tipping, farmer-killing city slicker.'"

I groaned. "Ugh. That's a new low. I'll be there in a few …"

CHAPTER 14

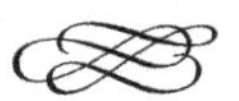

The setting sun painted ribbons of pastels throughout the cafe, turning everything golden and soft. I slumped behind the counter, scrolling through my phone while Hazel wiped down tables with more vigor than necessary.

I read another one of the scathing social media posts aloud. "This one says we put eye of newt in our Minted Mayhem Lattes, which is ridiculous. Everyone knows eye of newt is strictly for our fall blend."

Hazel snorted, moving to the next table. "My favorite's the one claiming we hold seances in the basement. We don't even have a basement!"

"Maybe they are referring to the old bootlegging tunnels under us."

The bell above the door chimed as Maggie Thomas, Pastor Jasper and a woman I'd never met walked in together. The cold winter air clung to their coats, which they shed and hung on the rack by the door.

"Hi everyone!" I greeted them with a wave.

Maggie approached the counter, concern weighing on her face. "Parker, I just saw those awful messages online. People can be so cruel!"

"Nothing I haven't dealt with before, Maggie. What can I get ya?"

Maggie smiled sweetly. "I'll try a peppermint mocha today."

I began preparing her drink and looked up to the others. "What can I get going for you, Pastor, and … I'm afraid we've never met?" I glanced at the woman next to him.

Pastor Jasper stepped forward. "Parker, this is Tara Joy, my better half. She's just returned from a mission trip abroad. I wanted her to meet you and try your famous coffee."

Tara Joy had wavy shoulder-length brown hair and wore dark-rimmed glasses and a vintage concert tee repurposed with scripture. A slender cross necklace hung delicately from her neck.

She smiled warmly. "Jasper keeps telling me your cafe is an answered prayer for Magnolia Grove. Thought I might try one of your famous blends."

"Nice to meet you. How about the Minted Mayhem? One part delicious, two parts chaos, just like life."

Tara Joy laughed. "Perfect analogy. I might use that in my next Bible study. Many times, the sweetest lessons come with a hint of chaos. I'll take a large one of those and a chocolate chip cookie."

"Perfect. Just came out of the oven," Hazel said.

I put the finishing touches on Maggie's mocha, adding a swirly heart design in the foam. "What'll it be, Pastor?"

"Please, Parker. Call me Jasper … I do enjoy those Mint Mayhems, but I'm in the mood for a hot cocoa this late in the day. By the way, Miss Hazel, you're still on for leading worship this Sunday, right? Everyone's excited to hear you sing again."

I looked up from my latte making. "I didn't know you sang, Hazel. You're a real Renaissance woman."

Tara Joy beamed at Hazel. "She has an amazing gift."

"Thank you, Miss Tara Joy." Hazel blushed, her mint-colored hair falling forward as she finished up Jasper's hot cocoa.

The bell chimed once more, announcing Nellie's arrival. Her waves cascaded over her shoulders as she bustled in with purpose.

"Evening, Jasper, Miss Maggie, Miss Tara Joy … I thought I saw y'all heading this way." She turned to the counter. "Hello, Hazel. Parker, honey, have you seen what they're saying about you on social media?"

"You mean the part where I'm supposedly running an underground cheese-smuggling operation?" I poured steamed milk into Tara Joy's Minted Mayhem. "Because I have to admit, that one's creative."

"I find that rather distasteful! That sort of attitude is such a blemish on our town!" Nellie insisted, her voice rising. "I wish, being mayor pro tem and all, I could summon the town's entire legal arsenal to defend your good name, Parker, but alas, I cannot and will not abuse my power—no matter how tempting it is to unleash my inner 'Lioness Lady of Justice' and scratch out the eyes of those trolls. Forgive me, Jasper." She smiled wryly. "By the way, I'll have my usual vanilla latte, half-caf, quarter pump of sugar-free vanilla, a splash of oat milk, three ice cubes and a dusting of cinnamon in the shape of a smiley face, and, of course, extra drizzle on the cinnamon roll."

Pastor Jasper chuckled. "Nellie, we're all grateful for your humility in leadership—and your restraint in not unleashing that lioness on unsuspecting citizens."

Hazel handed Pastor Jasper his hot cocoa. "Weird thing is, all these negative reviews came in at once."

Tara Joy accepted her Minted Mayhem and chocolate chip cookie from me, her expression thoughtful. "You know, this reminds me of the Book of Esther."

I blurted, "Sorry, I only know the CliffsNotes version of the Bible—Adam and Eve, Noah's Ark, Jesus and 'love thy neighbor.'"

Tara Joy smiled warmly with sparkling eyes. "No worries, though that's a good start! … Esther's one of my favorites. She's an example of courage and faith in the face of adversity." She took a bite of her chocolate chip cookie, then a sip of her Minted Mayhem, closing her eyes in appreciation. "Mmm, this is heavenly." Opening her eyes, she continued, her voice filled with conviction. "Anyway, a guy named Haman orchestrated a massive smear campaign against the Jews, sending letters to every province, seeking to destroy them. It wasn't random—it was calculated, deliberate and ruthless."

The word "coordinated" triggered something in my mind. The pieces started shifting, forming a new pattern …

"The timing of these reviews and texts," I said, starting on Nellie's favorite coffee drink, the coffee aroma filling the air. "They seem too perfect, too synchronized."

"Like someone's trying to drive you out of business," Maggie added, then sipped her drink.

"Or stop you from solving Walter's murder," Pastor Jasper suggested.

Or devaluing my business, I thought. I handed Nellie her coffee and cinnamon roll, extra drizzle.

I turned to Tara Joy. "What happened to Esther? Did she, uh, prevail?"

Tara Joy continued. "Esther's bravery saved her people. She stood up to Haman, exposed his plot and helped bring justice. Her story reminds us that even in the darkest times, courage and truth can triumph." She took a bite of the chocolate chip cookie.

Her words infused me with determination. I looked around at their concerned faces, feeling a surge of gratitude. The smear campaign might have knocked me off balance, but with friends like these, I wasn't going down without a fight.

Pastor Jasper checked his watch, then knocked on the counter. "Well, time for us to head out. Thank you for the drinks, Parker. And for being a bright spot in our town." He walked to the door and grabbed Tara Joy's coat.

"It's been wonderful to meet you. Your coffee lives up to its praise. As well as the cookie, Hazel." Tara Joy waved goodbye and walked over to Jasper.

Maggie gathered her things. "We're heading over to

Lauren's—see if she'll accept some support and prayer. Sometimes people just need to know they're not alone."

I bit back a snarky reply about Lauren possibly needing more than that, maybe an exorcism.

Instead, my thoughts shifted to Ethan's confession of his crush on Maggie just days ago.

"Before you go," I ventured, "Maggie, quick question—what's your opinion of Ethan Fontaine?"

"Ethan?" A hint of pink touched Maggie's cheeks. "The cheese-maker? He's … quite knowledgeable about his craft. Very dedicated." She smoothed her jacket. "Why do you ask?"

"Oh, no reason." I caught a slight flutter in her voice, filing it away for later.

Pastor Jasper paused at the door. "Hazel, see you Sunday. And Parker, our invitation for Sunday stands."

"I'll think about it," I said, meaning it more than I expected to.

The moment the door closed behind them, Hazel spun toward me. "Maggie totally likes Ethan."

Nellie dabbed cinnamon roll crumbs from her lips. "Lord, if those two get together, we'll have artisanal cheese at every church potluck." She licked frosting off her thumb. "Not that I'm complaining, mind you. So … Parker … anything new on the Walter Carr case? A little birdie told me they've got Lauren Yancey pegged dead to rights."

I sat on the stool behind the counter. "Oh, Nellie, ever the curious one, aren't you …"

"Well, I am the mayor pro tem. I have to keep my finger on the pulse of our town."

"That you do ... I think the whole thing might be tied to Walter's property. Any updates on what's happening with it? Legal-wise?"

Nellie set down her napkin. "According to the will we have on file, it all goes to Jesse."

"Wherever he is," I muttered.

"You didn't hear it from me, but there's a housing development company that just put in a bid on all the land surrounding Walter's. Town council hasn't given the green light yet, but the company is asking a heap of questions about Walter's property."

"Interesting ... What company?"

"Luminari Capital. They're out of Charlotte." Nellie stage-whispered, "Big money outfit."

I thought about the partially signed contract tucked away in my bag. My inner Whit-voice nudged me toward doing the right thing. Sometimes I hated having a conscience.

"Um, Nellie?"

"Yes, Parker?"

"Remember how you said Ronald Sweetwater was making a scene at the town hall, claiming he had a contract with Walter?"

Nellie rolled her eyes. "Lord, yes. That man was carrying on like someone had replaced his ice cream with frozen oil. Nearly knocked over my Ficus during his little tantrum in my office."

"Funny thing happened. I found that contract. Partially signed with a very specific stipulation about no developments."

Nellie's eyes widened, and she flipped her long hair over her round shoulders as she sat up straight. "Well, this is quite the development about no development!"

"Of course, I believe it's my civic duty to pass along the document. But would you mind if I hold on to it for a few more days?"

"What for?"

A small smile tugged at my lips. "I have a plan … to catch our killer."

CHAPTER 15

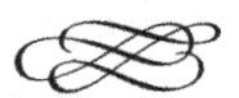

The last customer at Catch You Latte lingered in the reading nook while I wiped down the counter and equipment, clearing my throat occasionally to drop subtle hints that it was closing time. Whit, who had stopped by after work to help close up, offered a less subtle nudge, saying aloud, "Looks like it's just about supper time."

Finally, Mrs. Lewis, who had been immersed in what looked like a thousand-page novel, closed her book, stood up and stretched, her chamomile tea long gone.

"Thanks for letting me stay; I just couldn't put this book down!" She shuffled toward the exit. "By the way, don't you let all this nasty social media nonsense get you down. Your place is charming and so are you! Good night, you two."

The brisk January air rushed in when she opened the door, rustling the papers on the bulletin board and carrying the scent of woodsmoke from somewhere nearby. I locked up behind her, and the familiar click of the deadbolt echoed through the now-empty cafe. The cafe felt different after hours—bigger somehow and impossibly quiet except for the gentle hum of the HVAC system and the occasional ping from my phone announcing yet another one-star rating. I flipped around the sign to "CLOSED" and then returned to the counter to discuss my new plan of attack with Whit.

"Tara Joy and Hazel made a good point earlier—these attacks feel coordinated. The timing's too perfect. They all began to hit at the same time within seconds of each other."

A thought struck me. The Danger Zoners—those true-crime enthusiasts who'd become fixtures in my cafe during the Dylan Reeves case. What had started as a group of local college students enthralled by true crime had evolved into my personal tech squad. Hipster Holmes, real name Leland, and Ace, the Danger Zone Guy, had proven surprisingly useful, even if their enthusiasm sometimes bordered on overzealous.

Suddenly, the clattering of pans and muttered apologies drifted from the kitchen, where Hazel was attempting to clean up from her prep work.

I raised my voice over the racket. "Hey Hazel, can you come out for a second?"

She stepped out of the kitchen with flour on her apron and somehow in her hair. "It's not too bad in there tonight."

Whit and I exchanged glances.

I held up my phone. "Don't worry about it. Do you

think your study buddies could help track down the source of these reviews? Put those tech skills to work?"

"I'll ask. I'm going to see Leland right now ..."

"Oh?" I straightened a stack of coffee cups. "Thought you had class tomorrow."

"We're just studying. For class." I noticed the slight flush creeping up her neck. "Nothing else."

"Studying. Right." I caught Whit's eye as he collected empty sugar packets from the tables, and he bit back a grin. "And I'm just a simple coffee shop owner who never meddles in murder investigations."

Hazel reached under the counter and snagged the bag of Crazy Carl's jerky. "You mind?"

"Have at it. My jaw is still recovering."

She tossed it into her backpack before slinging the bag over her shoulder, nearly knocking over a display of travel mugs in the process. She headed for the door, leaving a trail of flour footprints in her wake. "We'll text you if we find anything suspicious."

Whit unlocked the door to let her out. "Have a good 'study session,' Hazel."

"You guys ..." She giggled as she stepped out into the cold night.

I poured a couple of mugs of my evening decaf blend, letting the subtle vanilla notes soothe my senses as I inhaled. The warmth of the mug steadied my nerves, a welcome anchor amidst the swirling questions. With all the talk about Walter's property—and now these investors from Charlotte—my gut told me *someone* I'd been getting a bit too friendly with *might* be tied up in this mess more than she was letting on. I needed to dig a little deeper and see how it all connected.

I handed a cup of coffee to Whit. "So, Nellie came by earlier and mentioned an investment firm down in Charlotte, Luminari Capital. They've been asking questions about the land around Walter Carr's farm. Coincidence that Jules works out of Charlotte?"

Whit took a seat on one of the stools, sipping his coffee thoughtfully. "Charlotte is the financial hub of our state, but perhaps you should give her a call?"

"Great minds think alike, Whit."

Finding Jules's number, I hit dial and put it on speaker. Each ring echoed through the cafe while my fingers danced on the counter, creating a nervous rhythm that matched my heartbeat.

"Parker Hayes." Jules's smooth voice carried that practiced cordiality she did so well, like honey drizzled over steel. "I was just thinking about you."

"Were you? How serendipitous." I perched on one of the bar stools next to Whit. "I've been giving your offer some serious thought."

"Wonderful! I knew you'd see the potential." Papers rustled in the background. "I'm touching base with investors tomorrow, but I'd love to discuss particulars with you beforehand."

"That's exactly why I'm calling. Due diligence, you know. I'd like to learn more about your investment partners. Get a feel for who I'd be working with."

"Of course!" Her enthusiasm sounded genuine enough to bottle and sell. "We're currently in talks to onboard with a great group. They're incredibly market-aggressive. Their entire philosophy centers around revitalizing underutilized areas through strategic development. They foster growth and innovation in local economies, creating iconic, design-driven habitats."

I mouthed "design-driven habitats" to Whit, who stifled a laugh into his mug.

"Sounds impressive," I said, keeping my tone neutral. "What's this company's name?"

A slight pause. "We prefer to keep our potential partner list confidential until things are finalized. But this deal is on the verge of being inked. I'm sure you understand."

"Absolutely." I straightened a sugar packet holder that didn't need straightening, watching my reflection in the darkened window. "Though call me paranoid, but if I don't know who I'm thinking of onboarding with, I just don't feel comfortable. I'm sure you understand."

The silence on the other end lasted two heartbeats too long.

"Understood. They are called Luminari Capital."

Bingo. The same group that was trying to buy up all the property around Walter's farm. Another piece clicked neatly into the puzzle.

Jules continued. "Well, what do you think? I'll sweeten the deal even more because I like you, Parker. How does a 7% stake in the joint-venture company sound? Conservative estimate would be two million. Optimistic estimate would be fifteen—for you alone."

My eyebrows nearly hit the ceiling. "That sounds very ... generous."

"Can I at least send you the paperwork to look over? No rush, but time is of the essence."

I'd heard many contradictory statements before, but none quite like that. The desperation beneath her polished tone was subtle but unmistakable.

"Email it to me. I'll go over it this weekend." I switched gears, keeping my voice casual. "How's Lauren doing? You talk to her?"

"I'm afraid she's not doing too well. I tried to give her a pep talk, but she didn't want to hear it. I think it's dawning on her that she might be going to prison."

"Maybe not."

Another silence, this one sharp as a knife. "Oh? You've found something?"

"I'm fitting together some pieces. Still working out the picture, though."

"Anything you'd care to share?"

"I promise I'll let you know soon. It's very precarious right now."

"Hmm. Interesting. Well, I look forward to seeing what you've uncovered."

"I look forward to sharing it with you. Send me the paperwork."

Her keyboard clicked in the background like tiny bones rattling. "Doing it now."

After hanging up, I turned to Whit. "Luminari Capital."

Whit finished off his coffee. "Doesn't sound like much of a coincidence ... So are you thinking this company or Jules are involved in Walter's murder?"

I rubbed my temples. "Maybe, maybe not. But they're

cunning enough to at least try to capitalize on the situation. Like sharks circling, waiting to attack when the moment's right. And Jesse's still our wild card."

"You think they might've fronted him money, and he killed his dad to get the farm?"

"Whit, I never underestimate the power of greed when it comes to treachery."

I pulled out my phone again, thumbs hovering over the screen.

"What are you doing?"

"Playing another card."

I crafted a text to Jesse: *I hope you're OK. Thought you'd be interested ... I found your dad's Promise to Sell document with Ronald, which would shut you out of the property ... How much are you willing to pay for it?*

The message showed as delivered, then "read." My pulse quickened, matching the rhythm of the blinking cursor.

"Whit! He's typing back!"

"Who?"

"Jesse."

He read the sent text. "I see what you're doing there. Making like you're going to sell him the document so he can destroy it. You and your lies ..."

"It's a ruse. That's not the same thing!"

We both stared at the screen, watching the three reply dots bounce like a pulse. The silence pressed in around us, broken only by the hum of the refrigerator.

Time seemed to stretch as we waited. The three dots continued their tantalizing dance ...

Then, abruptly, they vanished.

The screen remained still with an oppressive silence.

"I guess he's not interested?" Whit's voice was heavy with disappointment.

I frowned, squeezing the phone. "Maybe he's taking his time to think about it."

Or perhaps something more sinister was at play …

CHAPTER 16

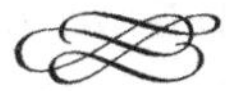

Main Street's charming storefronts glowed softly in the winter night, their yellow light spilling onto patches of glittering snow. Major trotted ahead of Whit and me, his nose working overtime, tail wagging like a tiny metronome marking time with our footsteps. The evening chill nipped at my exposed skin, making me wish I'd grabbed a scarf.

"I swear, every store owner in town has sent me their 'thoughts and prayers' about those horrible posts," I said, scrolling my phone. "Mrs. Pumpling even offered to send over her 'special' lavender tea. Pretty sure that's code for moonshine."

Whit chuckled. "Small towns. Everyone's in everyone else's business. They mean well."

"Bless their hearts."

"Hey, Southern girl! You're getting savvy with them idioms."

I kicked a little rock. "This whole expansion offer Jules

is pressing is off. The timing, the pressure … the connection to the financial company interested in Walter's property …" My voice trailed.

Major paused to investigate a particularly fascinating fire hydrant.

Whit's breath formed little clouds in the frigid air. "Might just be your infamous paranoia kicking in."

"More like my 'this whole thing stinks worse than month-old gouda' feeling." The words came out sharper than intended. "Sorry. These posts have me rattled. Twenty-three one-star ratings in two hours? That's not normal. And don't tell me it's just because I'm looking into Walter's murder."

"Nothing about this case is normal." Whit's hand found mine, his warmth steadying.

Major finished his hydrant inspection and bounded ahead, clearly proud of his contribution to the local news network.

My phone began vibrating.

Hazel's "study buddy" and resident Danger Zone computer whiz, Leland, popped up on the screen, his name accompanied by a picture showcasing his well-groomed facial hair.

I answered, "Hey, Hipster Holmes."

"Parker! Long time, no chat!" His voice crackled with excitement. "How've you been? Never mind, I know how you've been, Hazel filled me in. Anyway, I did a bit of digging into tracing those posts. Well, hold on to your coffee beans, because this is wild."

I mouthed to Whit, "Danger Zoner breakthrough," then

put the phone on speaker.

"We're listening."

Leland continued. "They're all coming from the same place. Different accounts, different IPs, but they're spoofed. The actual source is a property up by Lake Magnolia."

"You got an address?"

Leland rattled off a number and street name.

Whit's expression shifted to sharp interest as he said, "Parker, that's old Lakeside Hotel property."

"And?"

"It dates back to the 1820s. It's one of the oldest structures in the county. These days it's ..."

"It's what?"

"It's Jules Winston's winter cabin."

My stomach flipped over. "Did you hear that, Leland?"

"Already verified."

"How's Hazel taking this?"

"Confused."

"Tell her I'll figure out what's going on."

"You got it."

We hung up.

"Wow," I said.

"Yeah," Whit replied.

We stood in silence as Major circled back to us, perhaps sensing the shift in mood. The playful evening walk had suddenly turned into something else entirely.

I turned to Whit. "Feel like taking a drive?"

He glanced at his watch, then at Major, who sat looking up at us expectantly. "You want to go now? In the dark?"

"Best time to catch someone in the act, don't you think?"

Whit sighed, but I caught the slight upturn at the corner of his mouth. "At least we have Major for protection."

Major thumped his tail against the sidewalk, clearly pleased with his newly appointed security role.

"Come on." I tugged Whit's hand, steering us back toward Catch You Latte, where Bertha waited. "Time to pay Jules a surprise visit."

THE DRIVE to Lake Magnolia took us past empty fields silvered by moonlight, their snow-dusted surfaces broken only by pine trees reaching toward the star-speckled sky. Bertha's ancient heater wheezed valiantly against the cold, filling the car with the scent of hot metal and dust.

"Tell me more about this hotel," I said, fingers drumming on the steering wheel. Major sat between us on the bench seat, his head swiveling between the windows like a furry radar dish.

"The Lakeside Hotel started as a stagecoach stop," Whit began, his historian voice kicking in. "Built by the Montgomery family in 1823. The story goes that old man Montgomery won the land in a card game, but historical records show he actually—"

"Skip to the Jules part," I interrupted.

"Right. Turn here." Whit pointed.

I turned onto the winding lake road.

He continued. "Jules bought it five years ago. Restored

the main house but kept the original character. The historical society nearly had a collective heart attack when she painted it a different shade of blue."

"Oh, Mrs. Pumpling and the preservation police," I teased. "I had to arm wrestle her into approving my cafe's outdoor seating area—and convincing her my upstairs apartment wouldn't ruin the historic charm of Main Street."

"Still shocked you won. She was a formidable arm wrestler back in the day."

"Barely."

My phone buzzed.

A text from Leland appeared: *Activity still ongoing. Someone's running a program called "SwarmAttack.exe" ... Sending screenshots.*

"Smoking gun," I muttered, handing my phone to Whit.

Whit scrolled through the images.

"Question is, why would Jules want to tank my reputation? Unless ..." The puzzle started clicking together. "Unless she's trying to devalue the cafe. Make me desperate enough to take her offer."

Major suddenly stiffened, a low growl rumbling in his throat. Through the trees, a large structure loomed ahead, its neat facade barely visible in the darkness. No lights shone from any of the windows.

"Looks empty," Whit noted, his voice tight with tension.

I killed Bertha's engine, letting silence settle around us. "Jules's car isn't here."

"Maybe we should come back in the morning."

"While the evidence conveniently disappears?" I pulled

a small leather case from my jacket pocket. "I don't think so."

Whit's eyes widened. "Parker, no. Don't tell me that's a lock-pick set."

"Okay, I won't tell you." I opened my door, letting in a blast of cold air. "Coming?"

Major hopped out after me, his nose already working overtime. Whit muttered something that sounded suspiciously like a prayer before joining us.

The renovated hotel stood before us, looking less like a winter cabin and more like an extravagant lodge, its blue paint almost black in the moonlight. Neat columns flanked the front door, and a wraparound porch creaked softly in the winter wind. The gentle lapping of the lake echoed softly through the trees. The perfect setting for either a high-end bed & breakfast or a murder mystery.

"For the record," Whit whispered, "I think this is a terrible idea."

"Noted."

We approached the front door. No electronic alarms stirred, and no hidden cameras lurked in the darkness. Apparently, Jules didn't feel her remote winter retreat warranted any security measures beyond locks. I pulled out my pick set. The lock turned out to be a newer, top-rated model, probably upgraded during the renovations. But locks, like people, all had their weaknesses. You just had to know where to look. I began manipulating the lock's mechanism, and Whit watched intently.

"Want to know how I learned this?" I asked, glancing up.

"Not really," Whit replied, his brow scrunched.

Undeterred, I continued, "I had nightmares as a kid about being locked in rooms. My dad had the bright idea to get his locksmith friend to teach me. Dad said, 'Next time, pick the lock.' He gifted me this set." I smiled wistfully. "I slept with it under my pillow until I was twelve."

"Did it work?" Whit asked, curiosity flickering.

"Yep."

The lock clicked open with a satisfying snick. I pocketed my picks, ignoring Whit's disapproving-yet-impressed head shake. I eased the door open, wincing at the slight creak. I waited for any sounds of an alarm system and heard none. If there was a silent alarm, oh well.

"Still time to turn back," Whit whispered, glancing nervously over his shoulder.

"Major will warn us if anyone comes. Right, buddy?"

Major cocked his head, his tail wagging once, which I chose to interpret as agreement.

Whit caught my arm. "Parker, what exactly are we looking for?"

"Proof."

"What sort of proof?"

"Anything that could connect Jules to all this. Wait out here with Major. Text if you see headlights."

Whit's fingers tightened on my arm. "I don't like this."

"Neither do I." The admission slipped out before I could stop it. "But something bigger is going on here, Whit. That's a fact."

His expression softened. He pulled me close, pressing a quick kiss to my forehead. "Be careful."

"Always am." The lie tasted bitter on my tongue.

I entered the foyer, gently closing the door behind me. The interior was shadowy and smelled of lemon furniture polish and old wood. Moonlight filtered through tall windows, casting long shadows across hardwood floors. The place felt empty but not abandoned—more like a stage set waiting for its actors to return.

My footsteps echoed softly through the renovated interior despite my attempts at stealth. The grand staircase, now sleek and minimalist, curved up to the second floor. Rustic-chic accents blended seamlessly with modern flair, Jules's sophisticated style evident in every detail.

Old portraits, reframed in sleek, low-profile frames, lined the walls, their subjects' eyes seeming to follow my progress with renewed curiosity. Soft LED lighting highlighted the artworks, casting a gentle glow across the space.

A flicker of blue light caught my attention. Down the hall, a door stood ajar, the telltale glow of a computer screen spilling out.

Bingo.

The office space looked lived-in. Papers were scattered across an antique desk, coffee cup rings staining their corners. A laptop hummed quietly, its screen the only source of illumination.

I moved closer, careful not to disturb anything. The laptop's display showed an email that made me go *hmmmm.*

From: Marcus.Chen@LuminariCapital.com

Subject: Project Magnolia

Jules,

I'm already taking a big gamble on you since your financials are in the red. The board is growing leery. Taking too long to close. Too many hazards ... particularly with the landowner and your vested interests in Feta & Friends. Unless you can guarantee a secured acquisition on the Carr property in the next 48 hours, we're walking.

- MC

I opened the sent folder and found Jules's reply:

Marcus,

The Carr property acquisition is practically guaranteed. Just tying up some loose ends with the son, but trust me, he will inherit the farm, and he's already agreed to sell. The F & F situation will resolve itself once I transfer over proprietorship, pending Lauren's imminent arrest. Already have someone in mind. As far as being in the red, I guarantee my newest horse will win the blue ribbon.

- J

So ... turns out Jules was in cahoots with Jesse, all while cutting her losses with Lauren and handing over the reins to someone. And now, it seemed, I was her "newest horse" in the stable. What a mess.

As if things couldn't get worse, I noticed a program running on the computer, automatically churning out those phony bad reviews about me and my cafe. Then my eye caught a sticky note affixed to a contract with my cafe's name. In Jules's neat, unmistakable handwriting, it read: "Carr/Sweetwater Promise to Sell document with nosey cafe owner."

Seriously?

I snapped some photos with my phone before it started

playing the Indiana Jones theme—the ringtone I used for Whit. I jumped when headlights swept across the front of the house, spotlighting the walls before plunging them back into darkness.

Someone had arrived.

I crept toward the office door, my heart thundering in my chest. My phone rang again. Through the window, I watched a sleek black Mercedes pull into the curved driveway.

I heard the sound of a car door opening, someone getting out, then the car door closing.

My phone lit up with Whit's text: *GET OUT NOW!*

I heard Major's muffled bark, followed by Jules's voice. "Whit Hawthorne? What are you doing here?"

Whit's hesitation was palpable in the silence that followed.

I slipped through the side door, grateful for well-oiled hinges, and into the biting cold. I pressed against the side of the house.

"I ... uh..." Whit stammered from the driveway, his struggle with deception evident.

I smiled inwardly. Whit's ironclad conscience made lying impossible. Mine, on the other hand, was flexible—situationally dependent, I liked to think. Self-improvement was ongoing.

Time for damage control. Rounding the corner of the house, I feigned nonchalance despite my racing heart. "Jules! Perfect timing!"

She stood on the front steps, keys dangling from one

hand, her dark outfit merging with the shadows. "Parker? What's going on?"

Major trotted over, pressing against my calf. His hackles were raised slightly.

"I needed to come by. I don't know if you've heard, but my cafe has been getting slammed with a bunch of scathing reviews. I'm worried it might hinder our deal."

Jules's perfectly sculpted eyebrows arched. "You could've called."

"My phone died."

Whit cleared his throat.

"I haven't seen any posts, but I wouldn't be too concerned about them." Jules's lips curved into a practiced smile.

"The timing is curious," I said. "Right when you and I are discussing a business opportunity ..."

Jules tilted her head slightly. "That is curious ..."

We shared a charged, uncomfortable moment of "I know that you know that I know" before Jules straightened her shoulders. "Well, I should head in. I would invite you, but I'll be burning the midnight oil. I hope you review those documents I sent you. No pressure."

Whit and I turned and started heading back to Bertha with Major close by my side.

"Oh, by the way ..." Jules called out from the doorway.

Whit and I halted, turning to look at her.

"Be careful," she said.

"Huh?"

"There's a power outage in town," she said.

I nodded and forced a smile. "Thanks for the heads up." Whit and I quickened our pace. "Hey, Whit," I murmured.

"No power outages since last year's big winter storm," he said.

"How'd you know that's what I was going to ask?"

We exchanged one last look. "Because I know you, Parker. And it sounds suspicious to me, too."

We quickly got into the station wagon, buckled up and drove away from Jules Winston's house.

CHAPTER 17

The drive back to town felt longer and more tense. Whit kept checking the rearview mirror to see if Jules was following us. She wasn't. Once his paranoia eased, I shared what I'd discovered in Jules's office.

"The emails are evidence she's up to no good ... The Luminari Capital deal is under threat, Jules is in the red ... Lauren Yancey hasn't even gone to court yet and Jules is already planning to transfer ownership of Feta & Friends to someone else."

"Who?"

"That part, I don't know. The email didn't say. My guess is Ethan, since he just got a percentage of the company."

Main Street loomed ahead; the familiar storefronts were eerily dark. No streetlights, no warm glow from windows, just an inky blackness broken only by the occasional headlights of passing cars.

We pulled into the cafe's back lot. "Whit ... The back door is open."

I parked Bertha. Through the darkness, the cafe's back door swung slightly in the breeze. Major's low growl filled the car.

"You sure you locked it?"

"Positive."

Whit reached for his phone. "Calling Colton."

"No time." I jumped out before he could stop me, my phone flashlight cutting through the darkness.

"Parker, wait—" Whit's footsteps crunched behind me.

We entered the kitchen, and the cafe's familiar scents enveloped me—coffee, vanilla, cinnamon. Major was at my heels, hackles raised.

"Whoever you are," I called out, steadying my voice, "the register's empty and the coffee recipes are locked away. So, unless you're here for a slice of cheesecake ..."

My phone flashlight beam revealed shoe prints smudging through some ingredients on the floor that Hazel had missed with the mop. The prints led to my makeshift office in the alcove and then back outside. Whoever had entered had left. The contents from my bag and file folders were scattered and strewn across the table. Major sniffed around the kitchen, following the intruder's path to the back door. His nose worked overtime, cataloging scents only he could detect.

"You know, Whit, I have a *sneaking suspicion* Jesse Carr is back from wherever he was and came by the cafe to snag the Carr/Sweetwater Promise of Sale document we borrowed."

Whit stood next to me. "Ya think?"

"Was that sarcasm I just detected?"

"Hanging around you too much … But yeah, it's proof that Walter was going to sell the land to Ronald."

"I'm guessing Jules is putting the full-court press on Jesse to hurry up and close the deal."

"Or maybe it was Jules who broke in …"

"Either way, we're on the right track."

"Should we bring Colton in on this?" Whit asked.

"We don't have concrete evidence, just speculation."

"No, Parker, I meant about the break-in," Whit clarified.

"Oh … Nah."

"Just 'nah'? What about the document?"

"They didn't take it."

"How can you tell from a cursory glance?"

I motioned for Whit to follow me into the café, where I beamed my light onto one of the shelves.

"I hid it."

Whit's flashlight joined mine, illuminating the shelf. "Please tell me it's not in the coffee grounds."

I snorted. "Give me some credit." I pointed to Major's favorite coffee tin.

Whit's eyebrows shot up. "With the dog treats? Bold strategy."

"No one's getting past Major and his beloved treats. Right, buddy?"

Major's tail thumped against the floor, his eyes fixed on the container with laser focus.

I reached for the tin, and he began scratching my legs.

"Down, boy. You'll get one. Just showing Whit our clever hiding spot."

Major relaxed slightly, but his gaze never left the tin.

Inside, beneath a layer of dog treats, the document lay folded.

"See? Fort Knox has nothing on a protective mutt and his treats."

I tossed a treat to Major, who immediately began crunching away.

"Parker Hayes." Whit shook his head, a mix of admiration and exasperation in his voice. "You're either brilliant or crazy."

"Why choose? I like to think I'm a healthy mix of both." I slipped the folded paper into my back pocket.

We went back to the kitchen and started cleaning up my desk.

Whit gathered up the loose papers. "You think either Jesse or Jules would've killed Walter?"

"At this point, Whit, I wouldn't be surprised ..."

Just then, Whit crashed into the trash can, spilling its contents across the floor. I shone my light, revealing Hazel's neglected trash.

"Oh, Hazel."

Whit and I quickly gathered up the rubbish, stuffing it into a bag. Whit hoisted it while I lit our path to the back door.

We stepped outside into the cool night air.

You don't realize how dark a night can be until all the lights go out.

A rustling sound in the alley froze me. "Sounds like someone's over there," I whispered to Whit, nodding up the back alley. He set down the bag.

I killed my light, and we crept toward the source of the

noise. Through the darkness, we could make out a car backed up to the rear entrance of Feta & Friends. Major padded silently beside me, his nose working overtime. A figure struggled with something in the trunk.

My heart skipped a beat. Was it a body?

The figure grunted, and something heavy thudded. My foot kicked a glass bottle, echoing through the alley.

"Who's there?" Ethan's fearful voice called out. "I've got box cutters!"

"It's Parker and Whit, Ethan," I reassured. We started walking toward him. "What's going on?"

"Setting up the backup power source," Ethan replied, cardboard thudding against the trunk. "Been telling Lauren we needed one. This outage prompted me to drive over to Pine Ridge and pick one up. This beast has a state-of-the-art electric battery."

My flashlight beam revealed a sleek gunmetal gray box with EnergyGuard emblazoned on its side.

"Need any help?" Whit asked.

"Sure. Help me get it out of the trunk."

The three of us heaved the generator free. The thing weighed about as much as my self-doubt.

"So, you just got here?" I tried to keep my tone casual.

"Yeah." Ethan sliced through the packing tape with his box cutter.

"Notice anything suspicious pulling in?"

"Suspicious, how?" Ethan's tone turned cautious.

"Anyone lurking?"

"Nope."

Major trotted over to Ethan, giving him a thorough

sniff. Ethan paused his box-cutting to give Major a quick scratch under the chin. "Hey there, buddy."

The cardboard box fell away, revealing the high-tech generator in all its glory.

Ethan began checking to make sure all the various components were present.

Whit grabbed the box, flattened it and headed for the dumpster. He struggled with the heavy lid.

"Let me help." I dragged over a wooden pallet, using it as a makeshift step. The lid creaked open, and Whit tossed in the box. Part of it got wedged under the lid.

I strained forward, trying to free the cardboard. I climbed further up the pallet to get better leverage. My phone slipped from my pocket, tumbling into the dark depths of the dumpster.

"Dang it!"

"I can go in," Whit offered.

"No, I'm the dummy." I hoisted myself up, over and in. Luckily, it was relatively empty. However, something metal rolled under my foot—a spray can, by the sound of it. I retrieved my phone and turned on the flashlight. It was red spray paint. Now, wasn't that something? The same color paint someone had used to vandalize the Feta & Friends booth banner.

I climbed out of the dumpster, spray paint in hand.

"Hey Ethan, where did you get this spray paint from? I've been looking all over for this brand."

"No idea what you're talking about."

I held up the can. "This isn't yours?"

"I'm a cheese-maker, not a graffiti artist," Ethan grunted.

"You know whose it is?"

"No clue." He pointed to the generator. "Hey, Whit, can you help me carry this in? Parker, light the way, please."

Ethan and Whit heave-hoed and lugged the trunk-sized generator through Feta & Friends' back door while I illuminated their path.

While Ethan and Whit maneuvered the generator, Major kept close watch, circling them with curious interest. His tail wagged whenever they grunted with effort, as if offering moral support.

"Where is everyone?" I asked.

"Haven't seen Lauren all day. Sophia left a little while ago. No clue where she is."

They set down the generator with a thud. My phone light cut out. The phone was dead. Really this time.

"Double dang it!"

"Double dang it?" Whit echoed.

"Ethan, can I put your new generator to the test?" I asked.

Ethan chuckled sarcastically. "Sure, once it's up and running." Ethan began the process of powering it up.

"I'll be right back," I said. "Gotta get my charging cable. Whit, will you be my knight in *shining* armor? I'm not a fan of the dark …"

We exited Feta & Friends, Whit lighting the way back to my cafe.

I entered the dark kitchen and made my way to the

counter where my phone cable was plugged in. I set down the spray paint can and grabbed the cable. Something nagged at my brain like a splinter—a detail that I'd overlooked ...

The Frost Fest. The red spray paint on the banner. Sophia's story about Jesse tripping over the cord. The space heater getting unplugged and turning off.

"Parker?" Whit's voice cut through my thoughts. "What is it?"

"Remember during Frost Fest when the generator ran out of gas?" I said slowly. "Sophia told me that right around that time, Jesse tripped over the cord at Lauren's booth and knocked out the power to their space heater. But the generator was out of gas ..."

"The space heater would've already been shut off ..."

"Exactly. Sophia didn't know the space heater was already shut off because she wasn't at the booth. She lied about where she was during the time frame when Walter was killed ... How could I have missed it?"

"Because we were focused on the two most obvious suspects ... Lauren, then Jesse. Sophia's alibi sounded plausible at the time."

"Details, Whit ..." I picked up the red spray paint again, turning it over in my hands. "She's the one who was in charge of the banner. Of course, she vandalized it. It's so simple. Am I losing my touch?"

"No, Parker. You're human."

"But was she working alone? Or was she working with Jules? And how does Jesse tie in? Were they all in on it together? I think we need to have another 'chat' with Feta & Friends ... friends ..."

CHAPTER 18

"Over here," Ethan shouted.

Back at Feta & Friends, Ethan led me to the sleek EnergyGuard backup system he'd positioned near the storage shelves, tucked between wheels of aging parmesan and a rack of specialty crackers. The generator purred softly like a contented cat.

"Special ordered this baby from Switzerland," he said.

I plugged in my phone, watching the screen flicker to life. A grin spread across my face.

Whit leaned against a pristine stainless steel prep table. "You're looking mighty pleased with yourself."

"Just setting the stage." I dialed Jules's number, my fingers steady despite the adrenaline coursing through my veins. She answered on the second ring.

"Parker?"

"Sorry to bother you so late, but are you busy?" I kept my tone casual, like I was calling to discuss business rather than murder.

"Just winding down, tying up loose ends. What's up?"

"I have some questions about the expansion contract. Little details I'd like to iron out. In person."

"Right now?" A hint of irritation crept into her polished voice.

I borrowed her line: "No rush, but time is of the essence."

"Can this be discussed over the phone?"

"No, it needs to be in person. Can you make it to Feta & Friends by 8:45 PM?"

A pause stretched between us. "Feta & Friends?"

"Power's still out. But Ethan hooked up a fancy generator. The place is lit up like a stadium."

"Uh. Okay. I'll be there."

I hung up and turned to Ethan. "Can you get hold of Lauren and Sophia? Tell them there's an emergency at the shop."

He nodded, already pulling out his phone. His fingers flew across the screen with surprising speed for someone who spent most of his time perfecting cheese cultures.

I typed out a text to Jesse: *I know exactly what happened. Feta & Friends. 8:45 sharp (as cheddar)!*

The cheese pun made me cringe, but when in Rome.

"Think Jesse will show?" Whit tapped his fingers on the prep table.

"He's a wildcard," I admitted. "But worth a shot." My fingers hovered over my phone screen before I sent two more texts—one to George Baxter: *We need your help lifting a generator at Feta & Friends.* Then one to Ronald Sweetwater: *Have info about Carr property, come by Feta & Friends ... And bring me a cup of Killer Chocolate Chunk, one scoop is fine.*

I fired off a quick text to Deputy Colton: *If you want to be a hero, I'll get you a confession. Come to Feta & Friends, but park in the back lot. Slip in quietly at 8:50 and wait for my signal.*

"Ethan, leave the back door unlocked, please," I called out.

"Sure thing." He glanced up from his phone. "Lauren's not happy. She's on her way, though."

By 8:43 PM, everyone had arrived like moths drawn to the only lit storefront in town. George showed up first, his tracksuit somehow making his muscles look even more intimidating. Ronald bustled in, clutching a cup of ice cream and handing it to me. I nodded with thanks.

"Don't you think it's a bit cold for ice cream?" Whit asked.

"Nonsense! It's never too cold for ice cream! How are you keeping it from melting, Ronald?"

"Got a backup generator." He turned to Ethan. "What are you running?"

"EnergyGuard X3000," Ethan said with pride.

"Nice. Got the 2000 model myself, which does the job, but I hear the 3000 is amazing."

Ethan gave an assured nod.

Jules glided in next, and I barely recognized her without the usual CEO polish--just casual clothes and a ponytail. She surveyed the group, analyzing what was happening.

Lauren stormed through the door moments later, with Sophia trailing behind, both looking equally annoyed.

"Parker," Lauren snapped, "what's the meaning of this?"

"Justice," I replied, taking a bite of the ice cream. "With a side of chocolate chunk."

Jules crossed her arms. "I don't have time for games."

"No games." I took another bite of ice cream, savoring both the rich chocolate and the moment. "Just answers. Starting with you, Jules, and why you launched that cyber-attack on my cafe."

Jules's perfect composure slipped for just a fraction of a second, like a crack in expensive china. "Were you in my house?"

"I plead the fifth." I savored another spoonful of ice cream, letting the tension build. "But pressure's a funny thing. Makes people do desperate things. Like trying to tank my reputation and make me desperate enough to take your deal."

"It's a tactic," Jules said.

"Especially when you have investors breathing down your neck," I said.

"I don't know what you're talking about," Jules said smoothly, but her manicured fingers tapped against her arm.

"No? Luminari Capital doesn't ring a bell? They're threatening to pull out unless you secure a certain ... farm property." I paused, watching her squirm as that sank in.

I checked my phone. 8:50 PM. I thought I heard the back door lightly open and then close. Right on time, Colton.

"George." I turned to him, grateful for his imposing presence. "I know you didn't kill your old pal, Walter. I just needed someone with intimidating biceps here tonight."

George rolled his shoulders, the movement making Ronald take a small step backward.

"And Ronald?" I raised my ice cream cup in salute. "Honestly, I just wanted some ice cream. I'll make sure Nellie Pritchett receives the Promise of Sell document you had with Walter." I looked at Jules again. "Looks like you're out of that land deal with Jesse."

She rolled her eyes. "I'll find other deals. I'm resourceful."

"Whatever, Jules. Why don't we discuss how you decided to use this whole murder charge to your advantage. Cutting ties with Lauren, which, I'm guessing, you've wanted to do for a while—especially since you didn't approve of her rubbing the locals the wrong way. And now, by sheer coincidence, you've got your next candidate for ownership lined up and ready."

"What?!" Lauren sputtered, eyes glaring. "After everything we've built?" Her gaze darted between Jules and Ethan. "Who are you putting in charge? Him?"

Jules's lips curved into a sneer. "No. Someone you've not valued as much as you should have. Sophia."

Sophia bowed her head, playing the role of humble employee to perfection.

"Sophia?" Lauren's voice cracked. "Have I undervalued you that much?"

Sophia shrugged, keeping her expression carefully neutral. "I just try to do my best for the business."

The bell above the door chimed, cutting through the tension. We all turned.

Jesse Carr stood in the doorway, looking like he'd wandered out of a Brooks Brothers catalog instead of his usual dive-bar habitat. His khakis held a crisp crease, and his blue blazer actually matched his polished loafers. His mullet was still slightly disheveled, though. Looks like he was a work in progress.

"Well," he drawled, adjusting his cuffs, "gang's all here."

"Jesse." Whit straightened up. "Where've you been hiding out?"

"The Grove Park Inn," Jesse said, smoothing his blazer like he'd been practicing the gesture. "Great spa services, I'll tell you that."

"Who paid for that little vacation?" I asked, though I already knew.

Jules shifted uncomfortably, her veneer starting to crack.

Jesse pointed at Jules. "She did."

Jules held up a hand. "I didn't have a choice. I was doing damage control …"

Jesse lifted his chin. "She told me to skedaddle out of town on account of my little stunt."

"Care to share with the others what this 'little stunt' entailed?" I asked.

"You go ahead and tell 'em. I got nothing to hide anymore."

I faced the group. "Okay, I'll break it down for everyone. Jesse planted that evidence in Lauren's apartment."

Jesse rocked back on his heels. "When I'm well into my

brews, I don't think so straight. Honestly, I don't recall much." He pointed at Lauren. "But I do recall that I thought you, City Slicker, were as guilty as sin and might go free on account of your fancy lawyer. But once I sobered up this mornin' and got myself to a meetin' and did some thinkin', I realized I was being played for a fool."

"By who?" Whit asked.

Jesse jabbed a finger toward Jules. "By you."

"Jesse." Jules's voice took on that smooth corporate tone she probably practiced in front of mirrors. "I'm not playing you. I'm trying to help you leverage your assets into a sustainable future through strategic partnerships and—"

"Uh-huh." Jesse cut through her business speak. "I wasn't done yet." He swung around to face Sophia. "I think you're runnin' a game on me as well. Consoling me at the Double Barrel. Tellin' me your boss was guilty but might get off. Slippin' me that key to the slicker's condo and even giving me cash to buy those rounds ..."

Sophia's mask of competent assistant faltered. "I don't—"

Lauren looked like she'd taken a punch. "Why would you do that, Sophia?"

"You don't understand." Sophia's voice climbed an octave. "Yes, I went to console him, but only because I felt badly for him. Sometimes, the death of a close family member can trigger confabulation, particularly when paired with alcohol-induced memory impairment. The brain tries to create a coherent narrative—"

"Huh?" Jesse's face scrunched in confusion.

I set down my melting ice cream. "Ah yes, our resident

psychologist, plying her trade. Here's what happened ..." I paced between the cheese displays, the sharp scent of aged gruyere mingling with tension. "Sophia, so many years of service. So much dedication. You would do anything for Lauren. And how does she repay you? Giving an arrogant, snooty newcomer on your little team a stake in the business—no offense, Ethan."

"None taken." Ethan shrugged, leaning against the counter.

"That's ridiculous," Sophia protested, but her voice wavered like old milk about to curdle.

"Is it? You're the master of human manipulation. You designed escape rooms—controlled environments where you could predict and guide every move like a puppet master pulling strings. So, you designed an elaborate one right here in Magnolia Grove. One which would land you in the driver's seat of this very shop."

My footsteps echoed on the polished floor. "You saw an opportunity, didn't you? Walter refused to sell to Jules because of her connection to Lauren. The tension between Lauren and Jules was building, not to mention Lauren's public feud with Walter. One big mess just waiting to be manipulated. First, you vandalized Lauren's banner at the festival, knowing that Lauren would retaliate. Maybe you even suggested Lauren's perfect revenge—letting Bessie, the prized cow, out. While Lauren was offsite, and knowing she was too prideful to admit she would stoop so low as to release the cow, you used that opportunity to kill Walter, then plant the gun in her purse."

"You can't prove any of this." Sophia's voice hardened like month-old mozzarella.

A broad smile spread across my face, and I stepped forward, unable to hold back any longer. "Actually, I can. The red spray paint can in the dumpster out back. Then you claimed your space heater was unplugged and went out when, in fact, it would've already been out. Since the generator had run out of gas. But you didn't know that, did you? Because you weren't there. Because you were busy killing Walter Carr. All to frame Lauren and take over Feta & Friends."

"It wasn't only that!" Sophia blurted.

"No, it wasn't, was it? You wanted to get on Jules's good side to guarantee the transfer of ownership. So, you got rid of Walter Carr to procure the property deal for Jules. But you didn't know about the Promise to Sell document, did you? Not until I told Jesse I had it. And obviously, he told Jules, who then told you."

Jules spoke up. "Are you suggesting I had something to do with this whole mess?"

"I'm not suggesting, I'm insisting."

"This is all very creative, Parker. But you have no proof, because I wasn't involved," Jules said.

Sophia stomped her foot. "What? That's not true. None of this is!"

I stepped closer to Sophia, bent down, and rubbed my finger along the toe of her shoe. The familiar scent of batter hit my nose. "Ahh, yes. I'm grateful that my assistant Hazel, for what she has in baking genius, lacks in cleaning up. You have on your shoe a combination of ingredients that can be found nowhere else on the planet except my kitchen floor. You were in my kitchen tonight looking for the document, which we know you didn't find."

"You don't understand." Sophia's voice cracked like aged white cheddar. "I did everything right. This shop was supposed to be my future! And how was my loyalty and tireless hard work repaid? By being overlooked." Sophia whirled toward Jules. "And then there was Walter Carr and his stubborn refusal to sell. I thought I was helping you, Jules, by getting rid of him!"

"I never agreed to any murders," Jules said flatly.

"You killed my daddy ..." Jesse's voice trembled as he looked at Sophia. "Just for some stinky cheese shop?" The room tensed, waiting for an explosion that never came. Instead, his shoulders slumped, defeat replacing anger. He pulled a key from his blazer pocket and set it on the counter in front of Lauren. "I'm sorry I tried to frame you. Truly am." He turned to Ronald. "Ronnie, I know you'll do right by my daddy's property." Before leaving, he turned to Jules. "Ms. Winston, consider our partnership done. No need to throw more money at me." He quietly ambled out of the shop.

"Colton," I called out.

Deputy Colton emerged from the back, his silver mustache twitching with satisfaction as he approached Sophia. "Ma'am, I'll need you to come with me."

Sophia's shoulders slumped, the fight draining out of her like whey from curds. "I need a lawyer."

"I know a good one," Lauren said, her voice tight. "But you'll have to find your own."

Colton pulled out his cuffs.

I patted Sophia's shoulder. "Looks like a classic case of narcissistic syndrome with a severe side of manipulation mania ..."

The jingle of handcuffs punctuated the silence. Through the front window, I watched Jesse climb into his shiny new truck that I assumed Jules had bought to butter him up. The engine roared to life, and he pulled away from the curb, leaving his demons—and maybe some of his guilt—behind.

"Well," Jules said, straightening, "this has certainly been an ... illuminating evening."

"Illuminating?" Lauren rounded on her business partner. "You were going to push me out."

"Business is business, Lauren." Jules's smile remained perfectly painted on. "We'll discuss the dissolution of our partnership tomorrow. And Parker?" Her gaze landed on me. "My offer still stands. Think about it."

The bell chimed at her exit, leaving behind the scent of expensive perfume and ruthless ambition. I'd think about her offer ... think about flushing it right down the toilet.

I picked up my abandoned cup of Killer Chocolate Chunk, now a puddle of chocolatey goodness, and finished it in two blissful slurps.

CHAPTER 19

Morning light filtered through Catch You Latte's windows, painting the empty cafe in soft gold. The "CLOSED" sign deterred my usual regulars, all except one.

Sheriff Sinclair sat at the counter, her beige uniform pressed crisp enough to slice cheese. Her signature ponytail was pulled back without a hair out of place. For once, her face wasn't weighted with disapproval while she nursed a cup of my darkest roast.

"Not bad, Hayes." She took another sip.

I wiped down the already spotless counter. "It's a new blend from Chile."

"Not bad on the case either. I wouldn't have pegged Sophia."

"Me neither. She played her cards with just the right amount of eager assistance and reverse psychology on me. And I fell for it. That's what makes it sting a bit." I straightened a stack of plates.

"Careful, Hayes. Admitting you got played might damage that bulletproof ego of yours."

"Don't worry about my ego, Sheriff. It's like my coffee beans—only gets stronger with roasting."

Sinclair rotated her coffee cup. "Here's a riddle you can solve: Why do you think Sophia wanted you on the case?"

"I've considered that. I think the only thing that eclipsed her desire to run the cheese shop was her obsession with making a puzzle no one could solve. I suppose I was a challenge to her, and she was arrogant enough to reel me into her puzzle, so sure of herself that she didn't think she'd get caught."

"Reminds me of your episode about that surgeon who hired a PI to look into his wife's murder. What was it —'Episode 37: Operating on Evidence'? Guy was so convinced he'd crafted the perfect crime, he wanted to watch someone try to solve it."

"People are interesting ... Wait, are you becoming a fan of my podcast?"

"There was a lot of downtime during my conference." Sinclair's mouth twitched. "And the hotel Wi-Fi was free."

The bell chimed, interrupting our banter.

Jules Winston swept in, portfolio in hand, exuding polished confidence and totally ignoring the "CLOSED" sign.

"Sheriff Sinclair." Jules nodded. "How's little Simon doing?"

"Sawyer," Sinclair corrected, her voice cooling ten degrees.

"Of course, Sawyer. My mistake." Jules smoothed her

jacket. "I trust the sheriff's department is running smoothly?"

Sinclair's blue eyes narrowed. "Smooth enough to process another arrest if necessary. Those online reviews that were traced to your property were pretty shady."

"Let's be clear about that *regrettable* situation." Jules set her portfolio on the counter with precision. "My business strategies might be aggressive, but they're not illegal. Perhaps my team demonstrated excessive enthusiasm."

I stood with my arms folded across my apron. "And was tossing a bunch of money at Jesse Carr part of your 'aggressive business strategies' too?"

Her smile never wavered. "I provided resources and accommodations to a grieving son. He needed a new vehicle. And the Grove Park Inn has excellent therapeutic amenities. Jesse needed space to process his loss."

Sinclair set down her coffee cup with a sharp clink. "And what about Jesse planting evidence at Lauren's apartment?"

"I had nothing to do with that horrible idea. That was Sophia's manipulative tactics in play. Jesse just fell for it."

I narrowed in on her. "Admit it. You knew what he did. Because you were awfully quick to usher him out of town that day ..."

"I knew nothing. But I will admit, as far as Lauren's concerned, I took advantage of her legal troubles because I thought she was guilty." Jules smoothed her sleeve. "Disruptions create prime conditions for those with vision. And Sheriff, we both know any allegations against me for Jesse's actions or Walter's murder would be purely circumstantial. My legal team would have quite a field day with that." Her practiced smile returned. "If anything, I was the victim here. Sophia played us all masterfully. Such potential, wasted on criminal pursuits." Jules opened her portfolio. "Now, Parker, about your expansion opportunity—"

"Seriously?" I planted both hands on the counter.

"Business continues, even in times of organizational turbulence." She slid a contract toward me. "I've adjusted the terms. Fifteen percent stake instead of seven. That's potentially thirty million in the optimistic projection model." Jules tapped a manicured nail on the contract.

Sinclair snorted into her coffee cup, shoulders shaking with poorly concealed laughter.

"Something amusing, Sheriff?" Jules asked.

"Just admiring your management style with what did you call it? 'Organizational turbulence'?"

Jules ignored her. "Parker, think about the possibilities. Your brand has remarkable penetration potential in multiple demographics. The true-crime angle alone—"

"Give me some time to think about it." I drummed my fingers on the counter. "Okay, I've thought about it. Here's my counteroffer: one hundred percent ownership and a billion dollars."

Sinclair nearly spit out her coffee.

"I see you're not taking this seriously." Jules gathered her papers with precise movements. "The offer stands until noon tomorrow. After that, well …" She shrugged one elegant shoulder. "Market forces wait for no one."

"Neither does justice," Sinclair muttered.

"A pleasure, Parker. Sheriff. Give little Spencer my best."

"Sawyer," Sinclair and I corrected in unison.

The bell chimed as Jules opened the door to exit. She nearly collided with Lauren in the doorway. The two women locked eyes, and Lauren's face twisted with disgust, as though she'd just sampled a particularly offensive cheese.

For a tense moment, I thought we might need to pry Lauren's perfectly manicured nails from Jules's face. The air crackled with unspoken hostility before Lauren stepped aside with exaggerated politeness. Jules swept past, her corporate armor showing the tiniest crack.

"Got to admit," Sinclair said, watching through the window, "that woman's got some nerve."

Lauren entered, shaking her head and wiping imaginary slime from her sleeve. "Like dealing with a snake wearing Louis Vuitton ... Good morning, Sheriff." She then turned to me, her usual sharp edges softening slightly. "Parker, I wanted to extend my gratitude for what you did." She placed an elegant wooden box on the counter. "Some of Ethan's finest selections. Including his new lavender-infused gouda—strictly experimental, not even on the shelves yet."

"Lauren Yancey bringing me a gift? Did I fall into some parallel universe?"

"Don't get used to it. I realize I haven't been the most ... neighborly presence. I intend to work on that." She squared her shoulders. "By the way, Sheriff, will you be pressing charges against Jesse?"

The question hung in the air like steam over a fresh coffee.

Sinclair inhaled deeply, her fingers tapping against her cup. “Still weighing the options. Had a talk with him this morning. Boy seems genuinely interested in cleaning up his act.” She studied Lauren. “What’s your take? You’re welcome to press charges yourself.”

Lauren’s facade cracked slightly. “I just want to put this whole mess behind me.” She waved her hand dismissively, but I caught the hint of genuine empathy beneath her practiced indifference.

“Wait a minute.” I leaned forward. “Is Lauren Yancey showing actual compassion? Should I check for signs of the apocalypse?”

“Please.” Lauren rolled her eyes, but a ghost of a smile played at her lips. “I simply don’t have time for petty vengeance. I have a business to run.” She turned toward the door, then paused. “Though if either of you breathes a word about me being ‘compassionate,’ I’ll personally ensure your coffee supply is replaced with instant decaf.”

The bell chimed her exit, and I caught the definite trace of a smirk before she disappeared.

“Well,” I said, picking up Sinclair’s empty cup, “looks like miracles do happen. Even the resident ice queen can thaw.”

Sinclair stood, adjusting her utility belt. “Speaking of miracles, try to stay out of trouble for at least a week, Hayes. My paperwork pile’s reaching critical mass.”

“No promises, Sheriff. But I’ll do my best to keep the body count down.”

She headed for the door, then turned back. "That Chilean roast is good."

"I knew it! You're becoming a coffee snob."

"Don't push it, Hayes."

The bell chimed one final time. Through the window, morning sunlight caught the edges of my "CLOSED" sign, turning it golden. Time to flip it to "OPEN" and face whatever new adventures Magnolia Grove had in store. Though, hopefully, the next one wouldn't involve quite so much cheese-related drama.

CHAPTER 20

From my prime spot on the shore of Lake Magnolia, I dispensed steaming cups of my special edition Walter Carr Memorial blend—dark roast with hints of chocolate and cinnamon—to a gathering crowd of mourners-turned-Polar-Plunge-participants/spectators. Clyde had rigged up a portable heater next to my coffee station, both powered by a small generator he'd brought along.

"TELL me again why we're out here freezing to death?" I asked Whit, handing him a cup of coffee.

His blue robe made him look like a shivering monk. "Because George here wouldn't stop badgering everyone about honoring Walter the proper way … and, of course, breaking his record."

"Seven minutes, forty-nine seconds, that's the time to

beat," George proclaimed, his chest puffing out beneath his "Baxter's Blue Ridge Bootcamp" hoodie.

I handed another cup to Maggie, who'd paired her modest one-piece with a floral swim cap and a pink fluffy robe. Ethan Fontaine hovered near the coffee station, stealing glances at her.

Major sat beside my portable coffee station, sporting a little black-and-white-striped sweater. Nellie had insisted he needed to look "official" for his role as referee. His tail thumped against the frozen ground every time someone grabbed a cup of coffee.

Nellie bent down and petted Major. "Such a handsome sweater!"

"My sister knit it," Clyde announced proudly, adjusting the portable heater he'd rigged up next to my coffee station. Like me, he refused to join the plunge. He claimed his old bones had "enough sense to stay dry," but he'd shown up early to help set up and make sure we had enough power for the coffee station.

"Water temperature check!" Nellie called out to the EMT crew standing by.

"Thirty-seven degrees!"

"Thirty-seven?" Hazel cried out, standing among the Polar Plunge participants, her mint-colored hair clashing magnificently with her purple robe. Despite my best attempts to talk her out of this madness, my usually sensible assistant had caught the Polar Plunge fever. "That's like … really cold, right?"

Jackson Beauregard, wrapped in what had to be the world's most expensive robe, managed to look annoyingly dapper despite the cold. "Makes your typical board meeting feel downright cozy in comparison. And trust me, I've sat through some frigid ones."

Pastor Jasper, sporting a brown robe, cleared his throat, drawing everyone's attention. He stood at the edge of the shore, his usual warm smile in place despite the chill.

"Friends, I'm freezing already, so let's get this started ... We're gathered here today to honor Walter Carr—dairy farmer extraordinaire, reigning Polar Plunge champion and proof that stubbornness is indeed a renewable resource."

A ripple of laughter moved through the small gathering. Even Jesse, standing off to the side with Amber, cracked a smile.

Pastor Jasper continued. "Walter never met a challenge he didn't like or a cow he couldn't name. He believed in tradition, hard work and the absolutely insane idea that jumping into a freezing lake made perfect sense."

More chuckles. I caught sight of Ronald Sweetwater near the back, nodding along. The ink on his purchase agreement for the farm was barely dry, but he'd already promised to keep it running as a dairy operation. "No developments," he'd sworn. "Just ice cream, cheese and maybe a brewery."

"So today," Pastor Jasper's voice softened, "we honor Walter the way he'd want—by proving that Magnolia Grove's collective sanity is still questionable at best. Jesse, you may proceed."

Jesse and Amber stepped forward and walked onto the little dock, a small urn in Jesse's hands catching the sunlight. Amber squeezed his arm gently, wearing what appeared to be Jesse's letterman jacket from high school.

"Well, Pop." Jesse's voice carried across the water. "Guess this is your last plunge." He unscrewed the lid, his hands steady. "Try not to critique anyone's form from up there."

A gust of wind swept across the lake, catching some of the ashes as Jesse scattered them. The gray swirls danced over the water before settling on the surface.

"Bless his heart," Nellie muttered beside me, dabbing at her eyes with a handkerchief. "Even his ashes are stubborn."

The lake rippled gently in the winter sunlight. A respectful silence settled over the gathered crowd, broken only by the soft lapping of water against the shore.

Nellie straightened her shoulders, tucking away her handkerchief with efficiency. "Well! Walter would be kickin' up a fuss if he saw us all standing around like cold molasses crying all day long, so place your bets, folks!" She whipped out her official timekeeper's stopwatch. "Winner gets a free cheese board from Lauren's shop!"

Lauren, bundled in what looked like half of Nordstrom's winter collection, rolled her eyes. "I don't recall agreeing to that."

Nellie's voice cut through the chattering. "Alright, plungers! In position!"

Whit, Jackson, Maggie, George, Hazel and Pastor Jasper shed their robes and lined up on the dock.

"On your mark ..." Major's tail thumped excitedly. "Get set ..."

"Wait!" Hazel yelped. "What if there are, like, ice sharks?"

"GO!"

Six bodies hit the water with varying degrees of dignity. Jackson's perfectly executed dive contrasted beautifully with Pastor Jasper's "Jesus take the wheel" belly flop.

The first screams could probably be heard in Charlotte.

"Sweet mother of maple syrup!" Whit surfaced first, his usual composure shattered by shock. "This was a terrible idea!"

"Ooh my!" Maggie called out, her teeth chattering.

I poured more coffee, fighting back laughter as Pastor Jasper quoted scripture through blue lips. "'The w-waters c-covered their adversaries; n-not one of them survived.' Feels about right!"

"Jasper, honey!" his wife, Tara Joy, called from shore. "Don't forget to breathe!"

Nellie checked her stopwatch with excessive enthusiasm. "One minute in! How's everyone feeling?"

A chorus of creative expressions ranging from "peachy keen" to something that would make a sailor blush answered back. Major barked encouragement from his judging position, his tail still keeping perfect time.

"Giving up already?" George taunted as Whit made a desperate dash for shore. "Water's fine!"

"The water," Whit panted, accepting the towel I held out, "is anything but fine. It's homicidal." He huddled next to my coffee station, dripping and shivering. "Pretty sure I just saw my life flash before my eyes. Lots of dusty books and historical documents."

"First one out, does that count for anything?" I smirked, handing him a steaming cup of the dark roast.

Jackson emerged next, somehow managing to make hypothermia look stylish. "I prefer my business ventures without frostbite." He shivered, wrapping himself in a monogrammed towel.

Pastor Jasper followed, scrambling onto the shore. Tara Joy met him with the towel and a thermos of my coffee. "Here, honey. I have to say, watching your belly flop might be the highlight of my year. Very graceful." She wrapped the towel around his shoulders with a wink.

"Three minutes!" Nellie announced. "We're down to three participants!"

Hazel's mint hair had turned a deeper shade of sea foam from the water. "I can't feel my everything!" she wailed. "But I'm not letting you win, George!"

"Honey," Maggie called over, still serenely floating, "pride goeth before hypothermia."

"Four minutes!" Nellie's voice rang out. "Any predictions on our winner? I've got money on our underdog, Maggie Thomas."

"My money's on George," Clyde chimed in, fiddling with the heater. "Man's got more stubbornness than a mule with a grudge. Though I suspect Miss Maggie might surprise us all."

Maggie sang out, somehow still managing to sound cheerful, "If anyone's curious, my odds just improved." She nodded toward Hazel, who was making a break for shore with the speed of someone who'd just remembered feeling was a thing.

"I regret everything!" Hazel declared, teeth chattering as she accepted my offering of coffee and a towel.

George's determined stoicism had developed a distinct shake. "This ain't so bad," he insisted, though his voice wobbled more than his workout promises. "Just like my morning cold shower routine."

"Sure," I called out, preparing a fresh cup for his inevitable surrender. "Because that's totally the same thing."

"Five minutes!" Nellie announced.

"Maggie Thomas," George called out, his voice a mix of admiration and desperation, "what's your secret?"

"Prayer and positive thinking!" Maggie replied, executing a perfect backstroke.

"She's been practicing in her hot tub," Lauren informed us, wrapping her cashmere scarf tighter. "Had Ethan install a chiller system."

"Technically," Maggie's voice carried across the water, "that's called strategic preparation. And I'm sure Walter would appreciate the dedication."

The look on George's face shifted from determination to something close to respect. With a final yell and what sounded like a prayer for feeling to return to his extremities, he made his way to the shore.

"And then there was one!" Nellie checked her stopwatch triumphantly. "Six minutes and counting! Just one minute, forty-nine more seconds to tie Walter's record!"

"How's the water, Maggie?" Amber called out, snuggled against Jesse.

"Quite refreshing!" Maggie rolled into another perfect

backstroke. "Though I must admit, my lips are having a personal revival meeting."

Ronald Sweetwater wandered over to my coffee station, rubbing his hands together. "Mind if I have a coffee?"

"Not at all, Ronald." I grabbed a cup.

"Just wanted to thank you again for finding that farm document and handing it over to the town."

"Congratulations on your new ownership. How's Jesse feeling?" I handed him the hot coffee.

"He's holding up. Says he's changing his ways. Starting up a food truck business. I promised I'd do right by his daddy."

"Seven minutes!" Nellie's excitement could probably be heard in the next county over. "Forty-nine more seconds to tie!"

Major barked his encouragement.

"Come on, Maggie!" Hazel cheered, though she remained firmly wrapped in three towels and clutching her coffee like it held the secrets to eternal warmth.

"Forty-seven, forty-eight, forty-nine!" Nellie's voice cracked. "Ladies and gentlemen, she's tied the record!"

"Keep going!" George shouted, his competitive spirit intact despite his blue-tinged lips. "Beat his record good!"

Maggie rolled onto her back, raising one prune-wrinkled hand toward the winter sky. "This one's for you, Walter!" She kicked her legs, sending up a splash.

"Eight minutes!" Nellie's voice rang out with excitement. "New record!"

The group erupted in cheers. Even Lauren looked impressed, though she tried to hide it behind her scarf.

"And on that note," Maggie announced, making her way to shore with surprising dignity, "I believe it's time to render unto Caesar what is Caesar's, and unto hot coffee what is hot coffee's." Ethan appeared at the shore, extending a towel like a royal cape. "That was … impressive," he managed, his typical confidence replaced by shy admiration. "I, uh, kept it warm for you."

"How thoughtful." Maggie smiled, accepting both the towel and his hand as she walked out.

"You two aren't fooling anyone," Lauren muttered into her coffee cup.

I had Maggie's cup ready. "Congratulations on making Magnolia Grove Polar Plunge history," I said, handing her the steaming drink.

"Worth it." Maggie shivered, settling into her towel. She didn't seem to mind when Ethan stayed close, fussing about proper post-plunge temperature regulation.

Across the lake, Jules's fortress loomed on the opposite shore, its renovated facade a reminder of the chaos she'd tried to capitalize on.

"Hard to believe I used to idolize her," Hazel muttered, following my gaze while still huddled in her towel cocoon. "I even did my business final on her success strategies." She wrinkled her nose. "Had to redo the whole thing. Focused on you instead."

"Me?" I nearly dropped the coffee pot. "I'm hardly a business mogul."

"No, you're better. You build community, not empires." She nodded toward our gathered friends. "Though your coffee has world-domination potential."

Whit did jumping jacks. "I can't feel my feet!"

"That's what you get for jumping into a frozen lake," I teased.

Just then, a voice rang out from behind the gathering. "Well, hello, everyone! I made it!"

The group of shivering icicles standing around my coffee station turned to see Annabelle Beauregard, younger sister of Jackson Beauregard, walking toward us. She was bundled up in a luxurious coat with a man I didn't recognize by her side. He sported a designer ski jacket and a wide, accommodating grin. We were all surprised to see Annabelle, since she had vanished from sight after her brother Tate's tragic death.

Annabelle joined everyone. "So, when's this little ice swim starting?"

Nellie laughed. "Honey, sweetie, you just missed it."

Annabelle's rosy lips formed a pout. "What a shame. Where's Jackson?"

Whit chimed in. "Think he's warming up in his car. Where have you been hiding yourself, Annabelle?"

Annabelle's hand fluttered about. "After what happened to Tate, I needed to reconnect with my inner child and align my energies."

I barely suppressed an eye roll. "You've been on a retreat?"

"A world cruise on the *Celestial Oasis,* the most luxurious ship to ever grace the seven seas."

"Did you 'reconnect with your inner child' somewhere between the caviar buffet and the champagne fountain?" I joked.

The sarcasm sailed right over her head. "Absolutely! And that's where I ran into Truitt—my soulmate. We've been inseparable since Bora Bora." She linked her arm through Truitt's. "Everyone, you remember Truitt Ransom Treadwell? Well, after spending time in California, he's back home!"

Before I could respond, Jackson materialized at Annabelle's side, his expression tight. "Annabelle. Truitt? What are you doing here?"

Annabelle's smile chilled. "Hello, Jackson. We just stepped off the ship yesterday in Los Angeles and caught the redeye back into town last night. Thought we'd surprise you."

Truitt went in for a handshake and hug. "Jackson, how've you been?"

Jackson brushed aside Truitt's gesture. "What are you doing here, with my sister?"

Truitt's grin remained unfaltering. "Annabelle and I are together now, Jackson. Isn't that wonderful?"

Annabelle chimed in, "Jackson, I thought you'd be excited to see your ol' fraternity buddy …"

Jackson's jaw clenched. "No. And we're not buddies. Annabelle, we have family business to discuss. Meet me at Mother's in an hour." He turned to the group. "Everyone, good day." With a curt nod, he strode away.

Truitt's smile faltered, but Annabelle patted his arm reassuringly. "Don't mind him, Truitt. Lovely catching up, everybody."

With that, she sashayed away, Truitt in tow.

I said to the group, "How about we get out of the cold and go have a celebratory hot breakfast at Miss Pattie's?"

There was a collective "YES!" and Major was especially excited.

Everyone started helping pack up the coffee station. As I loaded up the back of Bertha, I watched Annabelle and Truitt drive away. My gut told me trouble was bound to follow those two, and I had a feeling our paths would cross again before long. But that was a mystery for another day.

THANK you for taking the time to read my book! There are millions of choices out there, so I appreciate you taking a chance on mine. Reviews are incredibly important because they help readers discover new books. If you enjoyed this book, please consider leaving a review—just a line or two would mean a lot to me!

TO CONTINUE SLEUTHING with Parker Hayes, check out the next installments on Amazon: Cafe Crimes Cozy Mystery Series. If they aren't available yet, they will be soon!

IF YOU HAVEN'T ALREADY, you can get my FREE ebook, A Sip of Suspense, about Parker's mysterious bus ride from the big city to Magnolia Grove when you subscribe to my newsletter: Simone Stier Newsletter or visit simonesti er.com. By subscribing, you'll be the first to hear about new releases, cover reveals, special deals and giveaways!

MY ACKNOWLEDGMENTS COULD FILL A BOOK. First, I'd like to thank my friend and savior, Jesus, for the gift of writing and for holding my hand through every storm. I'd also like to thank my amazing husband, Peter, for being the most wonderful writing partner and best friend. And many thanks to my family and friends for supporting my writing journey ever since I was knee-high to a grasshopper. And once again I'd like to thank you for reading my book!

CAFE CRIMES COZY Mystery Series

A Shot of Scandal
A Drizzle of Danger
A Blend of Betrayal
A Measure of Mayhem
A Sprinkle of Secrets
A Hint of Homicide
And more to come ...

LET'S STAY CONNECTED!

Simone Stier's Amazon Author Page
Simone Stier's Facebook Group

. . .

Simone Stier is a cozy mystery author who weaves tales of small-town intrigue, filled with charming settings and characters that feel like lifelong friends. Her stories draw inspiration from the quaint town in North Carolina where she resides with her husband and beloved dog. A passionate storyteller since middle school, Simone honed her craft by studying creative writing at the University of Maryland. A USA Today best-seller, she has shared her novels with readers around the globe. When she's not plotting her next whodunit, Simone leads Celebrate Recovery, binge-watches HGTV and dreams up delightful new cozy adventures.

Made in the USA
Columbia, SC
23 December 2024

50578074R00141